宝贝，一起读
双语胎教故事

睡前胎教 系列 SERIES

万娘娘（Wanderer）编著

中国轻工业出版社

前言

孕期最重要的是孕妈妈保持愉悦的心情,英语胎教不仅能带给孕妈妈科学的育儿理念、提升英语水平、获得轻松愉快的心情,还可以刺激胎宝宝的大脑发育、增进亲子感情,让宝宝提前熟悉周围的世界,对宝宝的成长是非常有利的。

研究发现,孕4月时,胎宝宝的内耳和鼓膜是其唯一已经发育成熟的器官。因此,从这时开始,胎宝宝就非常注意外界的声音,已经能够用耳朵去听。在胎儿期接受了英语启蒙教育的宝宝,在学校学习英语往往会更加顺利。

孕妈妈不用怕自己的英语发音不准,不用怕自己的英语水平有限,跟着英语名师万娘娘(Wanderer)学习,听老师读英语故事,带领胎宝宝一起走进英语天地,让他拥有更广阔的世界。

目 录

10　小乌龟和鸟
　　The Tortoise and the Bird

12　小马过河
　　Little Horse Crossing the River

16　给衣服的食物
　　Food for Good Clothes

18　小猫钓鱼
　　A Fishing Cat

20　湿裤子
　　Wet Pants

22　学会靠自己
　　Learning to Rely on Ourselves

24　999 片拼图
　　999 Pieces of a Jigsaw Puzzle

26　小牧童
　　The Little Shepherd Boy

28　再试一次
　　Try Again

30　龟兔赛跑
　　The Hare and the Tortoise

32　坏脾气
　　Bad Temper

34　三只小猪
　　Three Little Pigs

38　小猪噜噜搬西瓜
　　The Pig and Watermelon

40　狐狸先生与鹤太太
　　Mr. Fox and Mrs. Crane

42 愚蠢的驴子
A Dumb Donkey

44 乌鸦喝水
A Thirsty Crow

46 画蛇添足
Adding Feet to a Snake

48 飞行的乌龟
The Flying Turtle

50 幸福拍手歌
If You are Happy

52 下金蛋的鹅
The Goose with a Golden Egg

54 蚱蜢与蚂蚁
The Grasshopper and the Ants

56 老狮子
The Old Lion

58 狼来了
The Boy Who Cried Wolf

60 爱普莉月
April's Month

62 狐狸和小猫
The Fox and the Cat

64	狐狸和山羊 The Fox and the Goat	78	矮婆婆的树皮小屋 Grandma Short's Hut
66	狗、公鸡和狐狸 The Dog the Rooster and the Fox	80	想长大的小青蛙 Little Frog Wants to Grow up
68	守财奴和他的金子 The Miser and His Gold	82	傲慢的玫瑰花 The Arrogant Rose
70	谁是你的守护天使 Who is Your Guardian Angel	84	勇于承认错误的小象 Little Elephant Owns up Mistakes
72	老鼠嫁女儿 The Mouse Marries off His Daughter	86	小袋鼠让座 Little Kangaroo Offering Seats
74	小熊让路 Bear out of the Way		
76	顽强的小兔 Persistent Little Rabbit		

88 妈妈最辛苦
Mama Works the Hardest

90 鹬蚌相争
The Snipe Grapples with the Clam

92 拔苗助长
Pulling Up the Seedlings to Help Them Grow

94 南辕北辙
Going South by Driving the Carriage North

96 孔融让梨
Kong Rong Shares the Pears

98 猴子捞月
The Monkeys and the Moon

102 愚公移山
Yu Gong Wants to Remove Mountains

104 年的传说
The Story of Nian

106 东郭先生和狼
Mr. Dong Guo and the Wolf

108 田螺姑娘
The Snail Girl

110 守株待兔
Waiting for Rabbits by the Tree

112 十二生肖的故事
The Story of the Zodiac

116	聪明的小象 A Smart Elephant	132	晴天或阴天 Sunny or Cloudy
118	我的妈妈 My Mum	133	酸菜 Pickled Peppers
120	秋千 The Swing	134	季节歌 The Seasons Song
122	你是我的阳光 You are My Sunshine	136	来到车站 Down by the Station
124	我们同在一起 The More We Get Together	138	变戏法 The Hokey Pokey
126	萤火虫 Fireflies	140	回家路上不停歌唱 Sing Your Way Home
128	小鸟在说些什么 What does Little Birdie Say	142	动物园一日游 Going to the Zoo
130	纸船 Paper Boats		

小乌龟和鸟

一天,小乌龟嘲笑小鸟说:"你的家真寒酸!它是用折断的小树枝做成的,没有屋顶,看上去很粗糙。更糟糕的是,你还要花时间去修建它。而我的房子就是我的壳,比你那可怜的窝好太多了。"

"没错,虽然它是用折断的小树枝做成的,看起来很破旧,很粗糙,但是我亲手建造的,我很喜欢它。"

"它和其他鸟巢没什么区别,不可能比我的好。"乌龟说,"你一定是嫉妒我的贝壳吧。"

"恰恰相反!"小鸟回答说。"我的家里有家人和朋友的空间,你的壳却只能容下你自己。也许你的确有一个更好的房子,但是我却有一个更好的家。"小鸟骄傲地说。

The Tortoise and the Bird

A tortoise was resting under a tree, on which a bird had built its nest. The tortoise spoke to the bird mockingly, "What a shabby home you have! It is made of broken twigs, it has no roof, and it looks crude. What's worse is that you had to build it yourself. I think my house, which is my shell, is much better than your pathetic nest."

"Yes, it is made of broken twigs, looks shabby and crude, but I built it, and I like it."

"I guess it's just like any other nest, but not better than mine," said the tortoise, "You must be jealous of my shell, though."

"On the contrary," the bird replied, "My home has space for my family and friends, your shell cannot accommodate anyone other than you. Maybe you have a better house, but I have a better home." said the bird happily.

小马过河

小马和他的妈妈住在小河边。他生活得很快乐,时光飞快地过去了。有一天,妈妈把小马叫到身边说:"孩子,你已经长大了,可以帮妈妈做事了。今天,你把这袋粮食送到河对岸的村子里去吧。"

小马非常高兴地答应了。他驮着粮食飞快地来到了小河边。可是河上没有桥,只能自己蹚过去,可又不知道河水有多深。犹豫中的小马一抬头,看见了正在不远处吃草的牛伯伯。小马赶紧跑过去,问道:"牛伯伯,您知道河里的水深不深呀?"

牛伯伯挺起他那高大的身躯,笑着说:"不深,不深,才到我的小腿。"

小马高兴地跑回河边,准备蹚过河去。他刚一迈腿,忽然听见一个声音说道:"小马,小马,你别下去,这河里的水可深啦。"小马低头一看,原来是只小松鼠。

小松鼠翘着她漂亮的尾巴,睁着圆圆的眼睛,很认真地说:"两天前我的一个伙伴不小心掉进了河里,被河水卷走了。"

小马一听没主意了。

牛伯伯说河水浅,小松鼠说河水深,这可怎么办呀?他只好回去问妈妈。

马妈妈老远就看见小马低着头驮着粮食又回来了,心想他一定是遇到困难了,就迎过去问小马。小马哭着把牛伯伯和小松鼠的话告诉了妈妈。

妈妈安慰小马说:"没关系,咱们一起去看看吧。"

小马和妈妈又一次来到河边,妈妈鼓励小马自己去试探一下河水有多深。

小马小心地试探着,一步一步地蹚过了河。

噢,他明白了,河水既没有牛伯伯说的那么浅,也没有小松鼠说的那么深,只有自己亲自试过才知道。

金句拾遗

Real knowledge comes from practice.
实践出真知。

Little Horse Crossing the River

Little Horse and his mother lived by the river. He passed his days happily, and time flew by. One day, Mother called Little Horse to her side and said, "Little Horse, you're all grown up, and you can help mother with a few things. Today, you take that sack of grain and carry it to the village on the opposite riverbank."

Little Horse happily agreed. Carrying the grain on his back, he flew to the river. Since there was no bridge over the river, he could only wade across. But he didn't know how deep the river was. While he was hesitating, he lifted his head and saw Uncle Ox eating grass not far away. Little Horse hurriedly ran over and asked, "Uncle Ox, do you know if the river is deep or not?"

Uncle Ox straightened his big, tall body and laughingly said, "Not very deep, not very deep. It only comes up to my calf."

Little Horse happily ran back to the riverside and prepared to wade across. He had only taken one step when suddenly he heard a voice saying, "Little Horse, Little Horse, don't go in, this river is so deep!" Little Horse lowered his head, looked down, and saw it was Little Squirrel.

Little Squirrel raised her pretty tail with her round eyes widely open and said earnestly, " Two days ago, my companion accidentally fell into the river, and the water swept him away."

Little Horse had no idea what to do.

Uncle Ox said the water was shallow, but Little Squirrel said the water was deep. What should he do? He had to go back and ask Mother.

Mother Horse saw Little Horse returning with a lowered head from afar and carrying the sack of grain. She knew in her heart that he must have run into trouble, so she went to welcome Little Horse and ask about it. Little Horse told Mother what Uncle Ox and Little Squirrel had said.

Mother consoled Little Horse, saying, "Don't worry, let's go together and have a look."

Little Horse and Mother went back to the riverbank again, and Mother encouraged Little Horse to test out how deep the water was.

Little Horse carefully tried it out, and step by step he waded across the river.

Ah! He understood. On the one hand, the river wasn't as shallow as Uncle Ox said, and, on the other hand, it also wasn't as deep as Little Squirrel said. You only know if you find out for yourself.

给衣服的食物

一天，史密斯先生去参加一个晚宴。他穿着旧衣服进入了宴会厅，但是屋里的人都不看他，也不请他入座。

史密斯先生回到家换上了他漂亮的衣服，返回宴会。屋里面的每个人都站起来向他微笑，给他非常好的食物招待他。

史密斯先生脱下他的外套，把它放在食物中说道："吃吧，衣服！"

大家问道："你在做什么？"

他回答说："我在请我的衣服吃东西。当我穿旧衣服时，你们都不看我，也没有请我坐下。现在我穿上了这些衣服，你们就给了我精美的食物。我明白了，你们是把食物给我的衣服吃，而不是给我。"

Food for Good Clothes

One day, Mr. Smith went to a dinner party. He was wearing old clothes. He came into the room, but people in the room didn't look at him. They didn't ask him to sit at the table.

Mr. Smith went home, put on his good clothes, and then went back to the party. Everyone in the room stood up and smiled at him. They gave him very good food to eat.

Mr. Smith took off his coat, put it among the food, and said, "Eat, coat!"

The other people asked, "What are you doing?"

He answered, "I'm asking my coat to eat the food. When I'm wearing my old clothes, you don't look at me. You don't ask me to sit down. Now I'm in these clothes, and you give me very good food. Now I see. You give the food for my clothes to eat, not for me."

小猫钓鱼

  一只小猫每天去河边钓鱼,但他总是连一条都钓不到。

  一天,他像往常一样去了河边。突然一条鱼浮出了水面,他捉到了那条鱼,非常开心,却忘记把鱼放到篮子里去了。

  他又唱又跳,叫道:"我捉到一条鱼!我捉到一条鱼!"他所有的朋友都过来看。

  "你的鱼在哪儿?让我们看一看。"他的朋友们说。

  "在那儿,河岸附近。"小猫回答道。但是他怎么都找不到那条鱼了。原来,在他又唱又跳的时候,鱼跳回了河里。

金句拾遗

Every man has his faults.
金无足赤,人无完人。

A Fishing Cat

A cat went to the river every day to go fishing, but he could never catch any fish.

One day, he went to the river as usual, and suddenly a fish came up. He caught the fish and was very happy, but he forgot to put the fish in his basket.

Dancing and singing, he shouted, "I have a fish! I have a fish!" All his friends came to see him.

"Where is your fish? Let us have a look at it." his friends said.

"It's there, near the bank." the cat answered. But he could not find the fish. While he was singing and dancing, the fish jumped back into the river.

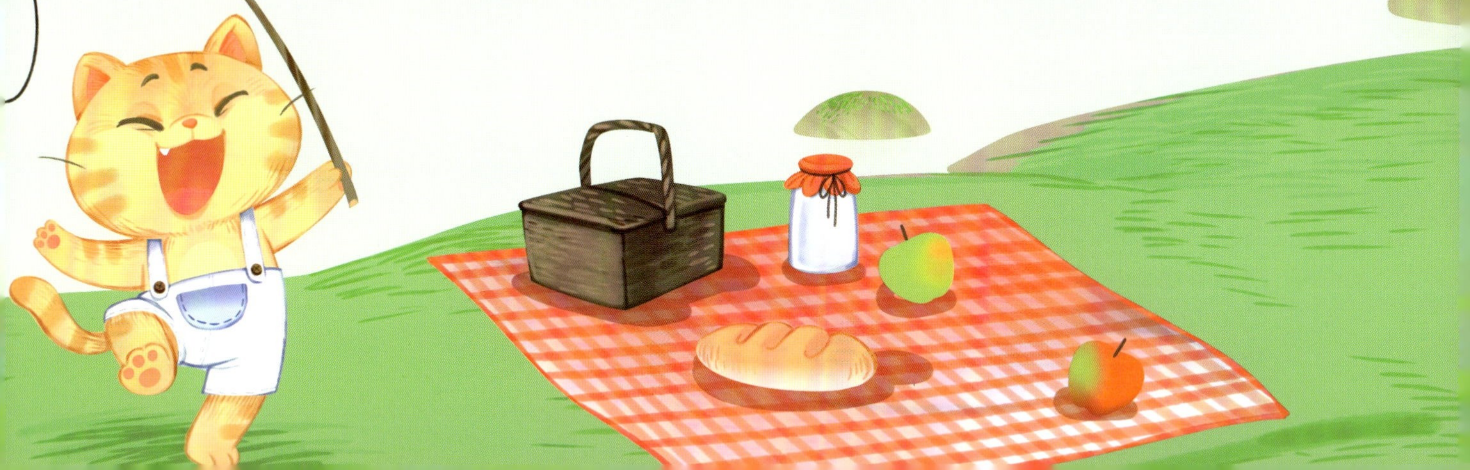

湿裤子

一个九岁的小男孩坐在教室前面的椅子上,突然,他的裤子湿了,脚边还有一个小水坑。他的心几乎停止了跳动,因为他担心同学们会看到并嘲笑他。

这时,他看到老师和同学苏茜向他走来,苏茜的手里捧着一个鱼缸。当他们走近时,小男孩以为老师注意到了他的湿裤子,突然苏茜绊了一跤,把鱼缸掉在了他的腿上。在感谢老天帮忙的同时,他假装生苏茜的气,并对她大喊大叫。

班上的每个人都认为是苏茜的错,是她把那个小男孩的裤子弄湿了。老师帮助小男孩换上干衣服,然后继续上课。

那天晚上,小男孩问苏茜:"你是故意的吧?"

"我也尿过一次裤子。"苏茜小声说。

Wet Pants

A nine-year-old boy was sitting in a chair at the front of his classroom. when suddenly his pants felt wet, and there was a puddle at his feet. His heart almost skipped a beat, as he became worried that his classmates would see and make fun of him.

At this time, he saw the teacher and his classmate Susie walking towards him. Susie was carrying a fish bowl. As they came closer, the boy thought the teacher noticed his wet pants. Then all of a sudden Susie tripped and dropped the fishbowl in his lap. While thanking God for helping him, he pretended to get angry with Susie and yelled at her.

Everyone in the class thought it was Susie's fault that the boy's pants got wet. The teacher helped the boy change into dry clothes, and the class continued.

That evening, the boy asked Susie,"You did that on purpose, didn't you?"

"I wet my pants once too." whispered Susie.

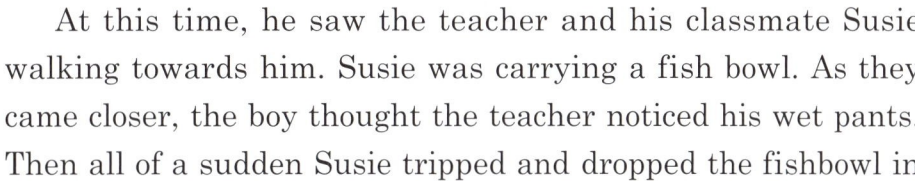

学会靠自己

小兔子住在森林里,他有很多朋友。一天,小兔子听到了野狗的叫声,他非常害怕,并决定寻求帮助。他很快找到他的朋友鹿,说:"亲爱的朋友,一些野狗在追我。你能用你锋利的鹿角把他们赶走吗?"

鹿说:"是的,我能。但现在我很忙。你为什么不找熊帮忙呢?"

小兔子跑去找熊。"我亲爱的朋友,你很强壮,请帮帮我,一些野狗在追我,请把他们赶走吧。"他向熊请求道。

熊回答说:"对不起,我现在又饿又累,需要找些吃的,请让猴子帮忙吧。"

可怜的小兔子又去找猴子、大象、山羊和其他所有的朋友,但没有人愿意帮助他,小兔子感到很难过。

他明白必须自己寻找出路。他决定藏在灌木丛下,静静地躺着。幸运的是,野狗没有找到他,就去追赶其他动物了。

须学会自己生存。

Learning to Rely on Ourselves

听 Wanderer 老师
读英文故事

Bunny Rabbit lived in the forest. One day Bunny Rabbit heard the loud barking of wild dogs. He was very scared. He decided to ask for help. He quickly went to his friend Deer. He said, "Dear friend, some wild dogs are chasing after me. Can you scare them away with your sharp antlers?"

Deer said, "Yes, I can. But I am busy now. Why don't you ask Bear for help?"

Bunny Rabbit ran to Bear. "My dear friend, you are very strong. Please help me. Some wild dogs are after me. Please chase them away." He made this request to Bear.

Bear replied, "Sorry, but I am hungry and tired now. I need to find some food. Please ask Monkey for help."

Poor Bunny Rabbit went to Monkey, to Elephant, to Goat and to all his other friends. He was sad that nobody was ready to help him.

He knew he must come up with a solution all by himself. He decided to hide under a bush, lying still. Luckily, the wild dogs did not find out where the bunny was hiding. They went chasing after other animals.

Bunny Rabbit learned that he had to learn to survive by himself.

999 片拼图

从前,有个叫切斯特的小男孩得到了一盒拼图。对于一个 6 岁的小男孩来说,1000 片的拼图太难了。但切斯特是一个聪明自信的小男孩,他相信自己什么都能做成。

这幅拼图是一个从窗口向卧室里张望的小女孩,她的眼睛好像正盯着桌子上的两只鸟在看。

切斯特从拼图的外圈开始拼了。不一会儿,窗户拼出来了,鸟儿和树拼出来了。慢慢地,小女孩的脸也拼出来了……但是等等!还剩一片拼图没拼上,他找不到小女孩右眼的那片拼图了。

切斯特看着完成了 99.9% 的拼图上的空缺处,纳闷那最重要的一片去了哪里。他开始在床下、枕头边找那块不见的拼图,甚至冰箱里也翻过了,但是始终没有找到。他很伤心,仿佛世界也不完整了。

"这是个 1000 片的拼图,我却只有 999 片。"正感到沮丧时,他把手放进了口袋。他感到有什么东西在里面:正是那片丢失的拼图!原来,那片拼图一直在他的口袋里。

999 Pieces of a Jigsaw Puzzle

Once upon a time, a little boy named Chester got a box of jigsaw puzzle pieces. For a six-year-old boy, a 1000-piece jigsaw puzzle is very challenging. But Chester was a clever and confident boy who believed that he could do anything.

In the puzzle's picture, a little girl was looking into a lovely room through the window. Her eyes seemed to fix on the two birds that were resting on the table.

Chester began to put together the jigsaw puzzle from the outer edge. Soon, the windows appeared. Then the birds and trees appeared. Slowly, the little girl's face appeared... But wait! The last piece of the jigsaw puzzle was missing, and he couldn't find the piece of the little girl's right eye!

Chester looked at the blank space in the 99.9%-finished jigsaw puzzle and wondered where the most important piece went. He started looking for the missing piece under his bed, underneath the pillow, and even in the refrigerator! But he could not find it. He felt very sad, as if the world was not whole now.

"This is a 1000-piece puzzle, but I only have 999 pieces." Feeling down, he put his hands inside his pockets, and there he felt something... It was the missing piece! It was in his pocket the whole time.

小牧童

从前,有一个小牧童以能机智回答所有问题而远近闻名。一天,国王召见了这个小牧童。

国王对他说:"我想问你三个问题。"

"哪三个问题?"小牧童问。

"第一个问题是,海里有几滴水?"国王说。

小牧童回答说:"我的王,将地球上所有的水都拦住,这样一来,我就可以在它们流入大海之前,数完数量,然后告诉您大海中有多少滴水。"

国王说:"第二个问题是,天空中有几颗星星?"

"给我一张大纸。"小牧童说,然后他用大头针在它上面扎了许多微小的孔,以至于看不见或数不清,使任何看着它们的人眼花缭乱。他说:"天空中的星星就好像是这纸上的洞,现在你可以数一数有多少。"但是没人能做得到。

国王随即说道:"第三个问题是,永恒有多少秒钟?"

小牧童回答道:"在波美拉尼亚下游,坐落着金刚山,高一英里,宽一英里,深一英里。每隔一千年就有一只鸟来,用它的喙(huì)在山上摩擦,当整座山都被摩擦掉时,永恒的第一秒就会消失。"

The Little Shepherd Boy

Once upon a time, there was a little shepherd boy who was famous far and wide for the wise answers that he gave to all questions. Now the King wants to see the boy.

The King said to him, "I want to ask you three questions."

"What are these three questions?" asked the shepherd boy.

"The first is-how many drops of water are there in the sea? " the King said.

"My Lord," replied the shepherd boy, "let all the waters be stopped up on the earth, so that not one drop shall run into the sea before I count it, and then I will tell you how many drops there are in the sea!"

The King said, "The second question is-how many stars are there in the sky?"

"Give me a large sheet of paper." said the shepherd boy, and then used a pin to make so many tiny holes that they were far too numerous to see or to count, and they dazzled the eyes of all who looked at them. This done, he said, "So many stars are there in the sky as there are holes in this paper, and now count them." But nobody could accomplish that.

At that the King said, "The third question is-how many seconds are there in eternity?"

The shepherd boy answered, "In Lower Pomerania is situated the Adamantine Mountain, one mile high, one mile wide, and one mile deep. A bird comes there once every thousand years and rubs its beak against the mountain. When the whole mountain is rubbed away, then the first second of eternity will be passed."

再试一次

这是你需要的一课,

尝试,尝试,再尝试,

如果一开始你没有成功,

尝试,尝试,再尝试。

尽管你会失败一两次,

再试一次,

如果你最终获胜,

再试一次。

如果你奋斗,就没有耻辱,

虽然你可能无法赢得这场竞赛,

这种情况下你该怎么办?

再试一次。

如果你发现你的任务很难完成,

再试一次,

时间会带给你回报,

再试一次。

其他人所能做的,

凭你的耐心难道不能吗?

只要记住这条规则,

再试一次。

金句拾遗

Never give up.
永不放弃。

Try Again

This a lesson you should heed,
Try, try, try again,
If at first you don't succeed,
Try, try, try again.
Once or twice though you should fail,
Try again,
If you would at last prevail,
Try again.
If you strive, there is no disgrace,
Though you may not win the race,
What should you do in that case?
Try again.
If you find your task is hard,
Try again,
Time will bring you your reward,
Try again.
All that other folks can do,
With your patience should not you?
Only keep this rule in view,
Try again.

龟兔赛跑

一天,兔子向动物们夸耀自己的速度。"我从来没有失败过,"他说,"当我奔跑时,没有人比我更快。"

乌龟平静地说:"我要与你比赛。""真是笑话!我可以一边跳舞、玩耍,一边和你赛跑,同样能赢得比赛。"兔子说。

比赛开始了,一眨眼工夫,兔子已经跑得不见了踪影。但是他觉得自己跑得快,就对比赛掉以轻心,躺在路边睡着了。

乌龟虽然慢腾腾的,但却持续不停地走啊走。当兔子一觉醒来,看到乌龟已经快到终点线了。

最终,兔子输掉了比赛。

金句拾遗

Modesty makes people progress, pride makes people lag behind.
虚心使人进步,骄傲使人落后。

The Hare and the Tortoise

The hare was once boasting of his speed in front of other animals. "I have never been beaten," he said, "for when I run at full speed, no one is faster than me."

The tortoise said quietly, "I will race with you."

"That is a good joke," said the hare, "I could still win the race while dancing and playing."

The race started. The hare darted almost out of sight at once. He soon stopped and lay down to have a nap.

The tortoise plodded on and on. When the hare awoke from his nap, he saw the tortoise was near the finish line and that he had lost the race.

坏脾气

从前有一个小男孩，他的脾气很坏。他的父亲给了他一袋钉子，并告诉他，每次当他发脾气时，必须把一颗钉子钉进篱笆的后面。

第一天，男孩在篱笆上钉了 37 颗钉子。在接下来的几个星期里，他学会了控制自己的愤怒，每天钉的钉子数量越来越少。他发现控制自己的脾气要比往篱笆上钉钉子容易得多。

终于有一天，男孩没有发脾气。他把这件事告诉了父亲，父亲建议他现在只要能控制住自己的脾气，每天就拔出一颗钉子。日子一天天过去，男孩告诉父亲所有的钉子都拔光了。

父亲牵着男孩的手，带他来到篱笆前，说："你做得很好，我的孩子。但是看看篱笆上的洞，围墙将永远无法恢复原来的样子。当你生气时说的话，也会留下像这样的伤疤。无论你说多少次'对不起'都没有用，伤口还在那里。"

Bad Temper

There once was a little boy who had a bad temper. His father gave him a bag of nails and told him that every time he lost his temper, he must hammer a nail into the back of the fence.

By the end of the first day, the boy had driven 37 nails into the fence. Over the next few weeks, as he learned to control his anger, the number of nails hammered each day gradually dwindled down. He discovered it was easier to hold his temper than to drive those nails into the fence.

Finally, the day came when the boy didn't lose his temper at all. He told his father about it and the father suggested that the boy now pull out one nail for each day that he was able to hold his temper. The days passed and the boy was able to tell his father that all the nails were gone.

The father took his son by the hand and led him to the fence. He said, "You have done well, my son, but look at the holes in the fence. The fence will never be the same. When you say things in anger, they leave a scar just like this one. It does not matter how many times you apologize, the wound is still there."

三只小猪

一天,三只小猪向妈妈挥手告别,他们打算独自去探索这个广阔的世界。

第一只小猪在路上遇到了一个拉着满车稻草的人。小猪买来了一包稻草,建了一个稻草房子。那天夜里,大灰狼来到小猪家门口,试图进去。小猪不让,大灰狼深吸了一大口气,结果把稻草房子吹倒了。第一只小猪见状,赶紧逃跑了。

第二只小猪在树林里遇到一个伐木工人。小猪买来了很多树枝,搭建了一个木头房子。那天夜里,大灰狼来到第二只小猪家里,试图进去。小猪不让,大灰狼深吸了一大口气,结果又把木头房子吹倒了。第二只小猪见状,赶紧逃命了。

第三只小猪找到了一些石头,"我要用石头盖房子",第三只小猪自言自语道。他把石头搬到一座小山顶上,建了一间石头房子。刚建完房子,他就看到另外两只小猪被大灰狼追赶,便向他们喊道:"快来我这里躲起来。"

两只小猪跑了进去,第三只小猪"砰"地关上了门,对大灰狼说:"走开,你这只大灰狼。"但是大灰狼不肯走,他深吸了一大口气,对着房子用力地吹啊吹,可是什么也没有发生。

"我来抓你们了。"大灰狼咆哮道,他顺着烟囱向下爬。三只小猪在壁炉上煮了一大罐汤,大灰狼从烟囱里掉了下来,"扑通"一声掉在了热汤里。

"噢!噢!噢!"大灰狼哭喊着飞快地跑出了小屋。

金句拾遗

Success waits on hard work.
成功来自勤奋。

Three Little Pigs

One day, three little pigs waved goodbye to their mother. They were going to explore the big, wide world.

The first little pig met a man pulling a cart full of straw. The pig bought a bale of straw and built a house with the straw. That night, the Big Bad Wolf came to the door, and he tried to get in. The first little pig wouldn't let him in, so the Wolf huffed and puffed and blew the straw house down. The first little pig saw this and ran away.

The second little pig met a man chopping trees in the woods. The pig bought many branches and built a house with the wood. That night, the Big Bad Wolf came to the door, and he tried to get in. The second little pig wouldn't let him in, so the Wolf huffed and puffed and puffed again, and he blew the wooden house down. The second little pig saw this and ran away as fast as he could.

The third little pig found some stones. "I'm going to build my house with stones," said the third little pig to himself. He carried the stones to the top of a hill and built a stone house. As soon as he finished building the house, he saw the other two little pigs being chased by the Big Bad Wolf. He shouted to them, "come and hide with me."

The two little pigs came rushing inside and the third little pig slammed the door. Then he said to the Wolf, "Go away, you Big Bad Wolf!" But the Wolf would not go away. Then the Wolf took a deep breath and huffed and puffed again, but nothing happened.

"I'm coming to get you," growled the Wolf. He climbed onto the roof and started to come down the chimney. The three little pigs were cooking a big pot of hot soup on the fire. The Wolf came down and landed – plop! – in the hot soup!

"Yow! Yow! Yow!" he shouted and ran out of the house as fast as he could!

小猪噜噜搬西瓜

春天的时候，猪妈妈带着小猪噜噜在山脚下种了一大片西瓜。到了夏天，西瓜地里结满了又大又圆的西瓜。

有一天，太阳炙烤着大地，猪妈妈对小猪说："噜噜，你到地里摘个大西瓜回来解解渴吧！"小猪噜噜高兴地说："好的！"

到了地里，噜噜挑了个最大的西瓜。他双手搂着西瓜，想抱起来放在肩上扛回家。

"哟，好重呀！"噜噜试着抱了几次都没有抱起来。突然，他看到小猴皮皮在滚铁环玩呢。

小猪噜噜一拍后脑勺高兴地说："有了，我有办法了。"小猪噜噜心想：铁环是圆的，可以滚动。西瓜也是圆的，不也可以滚动吗？想到这儿啊，小猪噜噜把大西瓜放在地上，咕噜噜地向前滚，一直把西瓜滚到家里。猪妈妈看到小猪噜噜把又圆又大的西瓜搬回家，她惊呼道："孩子，你真是太聪明了！"

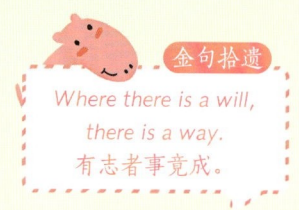

金句拾遗

Where there is a will, there is a way.
有志者事竟成。

The Pig and Watermelon

In the spring, Mother Pig took the little pig Lulu to the foot of the mountain. They planted some watermelon. When summer came, there were many big, round watermelons in the field.

One day, the sun was burning like a fire, and it was terribly hot on the ground. Mother Pig said to the little pig: "Lulu, go to the field to pick a watermelon and bring it back, will you?" Lulu said happily, "OK! No problem."

In the field, Lulu chose one of the biggest watermelons. Then he held it with his hands and tried to lift it onto his shoulder so that he could carry it home.

"Wow! It's so heavy!" Lulu tried several times, but he failed. Suddenly he saw monkey Pipi who was playing with a hoop.

Lulu patted his head and said, "I've got it." He thought, the round hoop can roll, and the watermelon is round, so the watermelon can roll, too. He then put the big melon on the ground and rolled it forward quickly. At last he arrived home with the watermelon. When Mother Pig heard the story, she exclaimed, "My child, you're so clever!"

狐狸先生与鹤太太

狐狸先生和鹤太太是好朋友。一天,他给鹤太太打了一个电话,诚邀鹤太太来吃饭。

第二天,鹤太太准时赴宴。可当她坐在餐桌旁时,她看到食物放在一个又大又扁的盘子里。因为鹤太太的嘴又长又扁,所以她是没有办法从盘子里吃到食物的,她被饿得眼冒金星。

第二天,鹤太太邀请狐狸先生到她家来吃他最喜欢的烤鱼。狐狸先生二话没说,马上到了鹤太太家。他在屋外便闻到了鱼的香味,"这是我最爱吃的东西,好饿呀!"

鹤太太从厨房里端出了鱼,可鱼不是放在盘子里,而是放在又长又窄的瓶子里。狐狸先生试着从又长又窄的瓶子中取出食物,可是舌头和嘴怎么都够不到美味的烤鱼。这时候,他认识到自己错了,羞愧地冲回了家。

金句拾遗

Easier said than done.
说起来容易,做起来难。

Mr. Fox and Mrs. Crane

Mr.Fox and Mrs.Crane were good friends. One day, Mr.Fox phoned Mrs.Crane and invited her to dinner.

The next day, Mrs.Crane came to dinner on time. She sat down at the table, but she only saw a wide, flat plate. Mrs.Crane had a long and narrow beak, so she could not eat anything from a plate. She was so hungry.

The next day, Mrs.Crane invited Mr.Fox to her home for his favorite grilled fish. Without a word, Mr.Fox came to Mrs.Crane's house. When he smelled the delicious fish from outside the house, he exclaimed. "My favorite food. I am so hungry!"

Mrs.Crane brought out the fish from the kitchen, but the fish was not on a plate. It was inside a long, narrow bottle. Mr.Fox tried to get the food out of the long, narrow bottle, but he simply couldn't reach the delicious grilled fish with his tongue and mouth. Then he realized his mistake and rushed home in shame.

愚蠢的驴子

一个阳光明媚的早晨,主人将一袋盐放到他的驴子的背上,他要到市场上去卖盐。

他们不停地赶路,走到小溪边时,驴子滑了一跤,跌倒了。主人帮忙拉起驴子,但驴子却发现它背上的东西变轻了。

第二天,主人在驴背上装载了更多的盐,并再度朝市场出发。可当他们走到小溪边时,驴子却故意跌了一跤,这次它自己轻松地就站起来了,主人失望地摇了摇头。

第三天,主人多放了些东西在驴背上,并对它说:"我们今天要再去市场,如果你跌倒了,你会后悔的。"

这是他们第三次来到小溪边,驴子再次故意跌倒。但这一次主人并没有帮驴子站起来,当驴子想要自己站起来时,却发现它怎么使劲也站不起来,它背上的东西感觉好重啊,比湿盐巴沉太多了!

这时,主人说道:"平常的棉花是轻的,可是湿棉花就很重。你的心思我早就猜透了!"

A Dumb Donkey

It was a bright sunny morning. A man was loading a sack of salt onto his donkey. He was going to sell the salt at the market.

They went on and on. When they came to the stream, the donkey slipped and fell. The master helped to lift the donkey, but the donkey found that the weight on his back was getting lighter.

The next day, the master loaded more salt onto the donkey and headed for the market again. When they came to the stream, the donkey fell down on purpose. This time he stood up easily, but the master shook his head in disappointment.

On the third day, the master put some more things on the donkey's back and said to him, "We are going to the market again today. If you fall down, you'll be sorry."

This was the third time they had come to the stream, and the donkey fell down again on purpose. This time, the master did not help the donkey get up. Instead, after a while, the donkey tried to get up by himself. Unfortunately, he found it impossible to stand up no matter how hard he tried. The weight felt so heavy on his back. It was much heavier than the wet salt.

Then the master said, "Plain cotton is light, but wet cotton is heavy. I knew what you were thinking!"

乌鸦喝水

一只乌鸦口渴了,他在低空盘旋着找水喝。找了很久之后,他发现不远处有一个水瓶,便高兴地飞了过去,稳稳地停在水瓶口,准备痛快地喝水了。可是,水瓶里水太少了,瓶口又小,瓶颈又长,乌鸦的嘴无论如何也够不着水。

乌鸦思考了一下,决定试着把水瓶打破,再把水瓶推倒,可是乌鸦的力量不够大,这个想法失败了。

乌鸦看见路边有许多小石子,便叼来许多,把它们一块一块地投到水瓶里。随着石子的增多,水瓶里的水也一点儿一点儿地慢慢向上升……

终于,水瓶里的水快升到瓶口了,乌鸦总算可以喝到水了。

就这样,聪明的乌鸦成功地喝到了水瓶里的水。

金句拾遗

Knowledge is power.
知识就是力量。

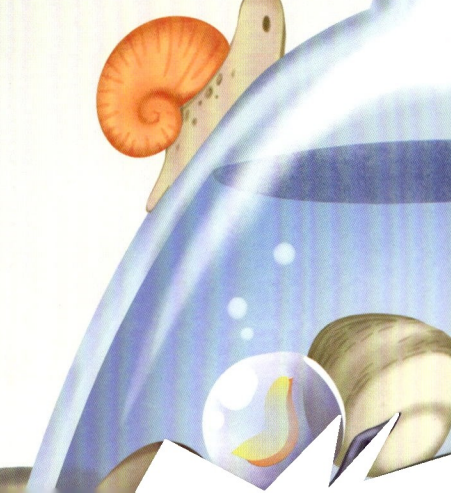

A Thirsty Crow

A crow was thirsty. He circled low in the sky looking for water. After looking for a long time, he found a water pitcher not far away. He flew happily to it, stopped at the bottom of the bottle, and was ready to drink. However, there was very little water in the pitcher, and the mouth and neck of the pitcher were so small that the crow's mouth could barely reach the water at all.

The crow thought for a while and decided to break the pitcher and then push it over, but this idea failed.

Then the crow saw many small stones by the side of the road. He took many stones and dropped them one by one into the pitcher. As the number of stones increased, little by little the water in the bottle slowly rose.

Finally, the water in the bottle was almost up to the top, and the crow could drink from it.

In this way, the clever crow succeeded in drinking from the pitcher.

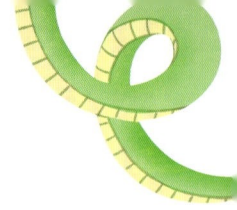

画蛇添足

一天,狮子先生举办了一场聚会,许多动物都来喝酒。当喝到只剩一壶酒时,大家犯了难,应该让谁喝呢?他们想了想,想到一个好主意:他们决定比赛画蛇,谁最快画好,就给谁喝这壶酒。

不一会,狼先生画好了。"哈,我画好了,我是第一名。"他说道。

"要不我再给蛇加几只脚吧。"狼先生补充道。

就在这个时候,猩猩先生也画好了。他拿起那酒壶喝了起来,一边喝一边说:"他画的那不是蛇,蛇是没有脚的,所以是我赢了这壶酒。"

金句拾遗

Prove futile.
徒劳无功。

Adding Feet to a Snake

One day, Mr. Lion held a party. Many animals came and drank wine. When there was one last pot of wine left, everyone was in a dilemma. Who should drink the last pot? They came up with a good idea and decided to hold a contest called "Draw a snake." Whoever finished first could have the last pot of wine.

Soon Mr. Wolf finished drawing. "Yeah, I've finished! I'm Number 1!" he exclaimed.

"But maybe I should add a few more feet," Mr. Wolf then said.

At the same time, Mr. Gorilla also finished. He took away the pot of wine and drank it. Then he said, "That isn't a snake. Snakes have no feet. I win the pot!"

飞行的乌龟

在一个阳光明媚的早晨,乌龟先生打算上岸去溜达一下。

"我已经厌烦整日游泳了,今天我要到岸上去。"乌龟对小鱼说。

"你真幸运,我也想看看外面的世界。"小鱼羡慕地说道。

乌龟骄傲地说道:"等我回来,我教你怎么飞。"

乌龟来到陆地,看见了老鹰,便对老鹰说:"你能带我上天去看看吗?只要这一次,我很想从天空俯瞰陆地和海洋。"

老鹰说:"那上面很危险,如果你掉下来怎么办?"乌龟说:"别担心,我会抓紧,我会小心的。"乌龟不断地恳求。老鹰说:"好吧,现在抓紧了。我们上去吧,一,二,三……"

乌龟说:"我的天啊!好漂亮,我要到更高的地方。"老鹰说:"那太危险了,我们还是下去吧。"

乌龟说:"这里实在是太棒了。我想现在我可以靠自己飞了。"老鹰说:"你疯了吗?你自己是无法飞翔的。"乌龟说:"不,我可以。我飞给你看,请放开我。"

老鹰将乌龟放开的那一刹那,乌龟便开始往下掉啊掉啊。"可怜的乌龟先生,我再也不羡慕他了。"小鱼哀叹道。

The Flying Turtle

One bright, sunny morning, Mr. Turtle decided to go ashore for a walk.

"I am tired of swimming all day. I'll go out onto the shore today." the turtle said to the little fish.

"You are so lucky. I want to see the outside world, too," said the little fish with envy.

The turtle said proudly, "When I get back, I'll show you how to fly."

When the turtle reached the land, he saw the eagle and said to the eagle, "Can you take me up to the sky for a ride? Just this once, I'd like to see the land and the sea from the sky."

The eagle said, "It's dangerous up there. What if you fall?"The turtle replied, "Don't worry. I'll hold on tight, I'll be careful." The turtle kept begging.The eagle said, "Okay, then hold on tight. Let's go up. One , two, three..."

The turtle replied, "Oh my goodness! It's so beautiful. I want to go up higher."The eagle said, "It's too dangerous. Let's go down now."

The turtle replied, "It is so wonderful up here. I think I can fly by myself now."The eagle said, "Are you crazy? You can't fly by yourself！"The turtle replied, "Yes, I can. I'll show you. Please, let me go."

The eagle let go, and the turtle started to fall down. "Poor Mr. Turtle. I don't envy him anymore." the little fish lamented.

幸福拍手歌

如果你感到很快乐，就拍拍手吧。

如果你感到很快乐，就拍拍手吧。

如果你感到很快乐，就大胆表露出来吧！

如果你感到很快乐，就拍拍手吧。

如果你感到很快乐，就跺跺脚吧。

如果你感到很快乐，就跺跺脚吧。

如果你感到很快乐，就大胆表露出来吧！

如果你感到很快乐，就跺跺脚吧。

如果你感到很快乐，就眨眨眼吧。

如果你感到很快乐，就眨眨眼吧。

如果你感到很快乐，就大胆表露出来吧！

如果你感到很快乐，就眨眨眼吧。

If You are Happy

If you're happy and you know it clap your hands.
If you're happy and you know it clap your hands.
If you're happy and you know it never be afraid to show it!
If you're happy and you know it clap your hands.
If you're happy and you know it stomp your feet.
If you're happy and you know it stomp your feet.
If you're happy and you know it never be afraid to show it!
If you're happy and you know it stomp your feet.
If you're happy and you know it wink your eye.
If you're happy and you know it wink your eye.
If you're happy and you know it never be afraid to show it!
If you're happy and you know it wink your eye.

下金蛋的鹅

有一天,农夫和他的妻子在谷仓里发现了一颗金蛋,这颗蛋是鹅生下来的。老两口很开心,决定把金蛋拿到市场上去卖。他们用卖金蛋的钱买回来很多肉和米。

那天晚上他们非常兴奋,以至于无法入睡,并且希望鹅在第二天会再生一颗金蛋。

第二天早上,他们冲到谷仓,发现鹅生了第二颗金蛋。"多亏了你这只鹅,我们很快就会富裕起来了。"

从那以后,农夫和他的妻子给鹅吃最好的食物,他们很疼爱那只鹅,而鹅也继续每天生一颗金蛋。几个月后,这对夫妻搬到了更大的房子里,他们的日子幸福而富足。

一天,农夫的妻子突然说道:"我想快点变得更富有,虽然我们不知道那只鹅怎么会生金蛋,但是我们知道那些金蛋是从它肚子里来的。我觉得它的肚子里一定装满了金蛋。"

这时候农夫上前抓住了鹅,剖开了它的肚子。可是,令农夫和他的妻子惊讶的是,鹅的肚子里并没有金蛋。

夫妻两人哭泣道:"可怜的鹅,是我们太贪心了。"

The Goose with a Golden Egg

One day, a farmer and his wife found a golden egg in the barn. Their goose had laid this golden egg. They were so happy about this and decided to sell the golden egg. With the money, they brought back home a lot of meat and rice.

They were so excited that they could not fall asleep that night, hoping that the goose would lay another golden egg the next day.

On the morning of the second day, they both rushed to the barn and found another golden egg. "Thank you, goose! We will be rich soon."

After that, the farmer and his wife gave the goose the best food. They loved the goose. The goose kept laying a golden egg every day. Some months later, the couple moved to a bigger house, and they were very happy and wealthy.

One day, the wife suddenly said, "I want to get very rich even faster. we do not know how the goose produces those golden eggs, but we know where they are from. I think its stomach must be full of golden eggs.

At this time, the farmer went up to catch the goose and cut open its stomach. But to their great astonishment, there was nothing inside its stomach.

The couple cried out loud, "Poor Goose! We were too greedy."

蚱蜢与蚂蚁

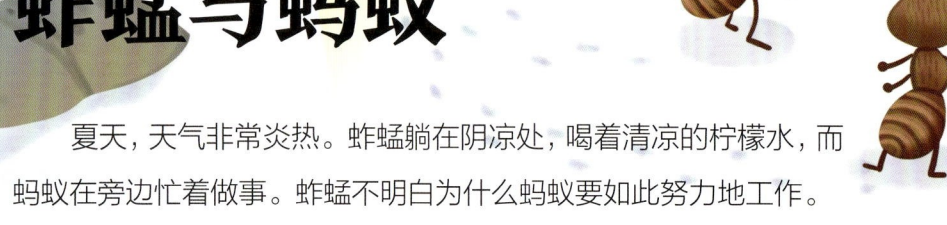

夏天，天气非常炎热。蚱蜢躺在阴凉处，喝着清凉的柠檬水，而蚂蚁在旁边忙着做事。蚱蜢不明白为什么蚂蚁要如此努力地工作。

蚱蜢问："嗨，蚁后！你们为什么要收集食物呢？"

蚁后回应道："冬天快到了，我们必须要有所准备。"

蚱蜢说："你在开玩笑吧！现在是7月，冬天还早着呢！别工作了，跟我一起唱歌跳舞吧！"

蚁后回答说："你应该收集一些食物。否则，在冬天你会挨饿的。"

蚱蜢不听，整个夏天，他没有收集任何食物。很快，冬天来了，蚱蜢在寒风中四处寻找食物。

蚱蜢心里想："蚂蚁们一定有很多食物。或许，他们可以帮助我。"

蚱蜢找到了蚁后的家，对蚁后说："蚁后，你可以给我点东西吃吗？拜托！"

蚁后说："嗯，好吧。在这里等一下。"

蚁后觉得蚱蜢很可怜，于是她走到厨房去给他拿了一些面包。可是当她回来时，发现蚱蜢已经冻僵了。

The Grasshopper and the Ants

Summer weather was boiling hot. The Grasshopper was lying under the shade and drinking cold lemonade. The Ants were busy doing something. The Grasshopper did not know why they were working so hard.

The Grasshopper asked, "Hey Queen Ant, why are you gathering food?"

The Queen Ant replied, "It will be winter soon. We must be prepared."

The Grasshopper said, "The winter?! You must be kidding! It is July. Winter is far away. Stop working. Come sing and dance with me."

The Queen Ant answered,"You should collect some food, or else you will starve in the winter."

The Grasshopper refused to listen, and during the whole summer, he collected nothing. Sooner or later, the winter arrived. The Grasshopper looked around for food in the cold.

Then the Grasshopper said, "The Ants must have lots of food. Maybe they can help me."

The Grasshopper found the Queen, "Can I have something to eat, please?"

The Queen said, "Well, okay. Just wait here for a minute."

The Queen Ant felt sorry for the Grasshopper and went to the kitchen to get him some bread. But when she came back, the Grasshopper was already frozen like ice.

老狮子

从前有头狮子,他曾经是百兽之王,可是现在却又老又孱弱。

有一天,兔子对松鼠说:"你听说狮子的事了吗?听说他病得很重。我们去看看他吧!"

他们走进了洞穴深处。可就在这个时候,狮子突然站了起来,露出了他的牙齿、伸出了他的爪子。

兔子惊慌地说:"我们快逃吧!"狮子对他们吼道:"太晚了,你们跑不了了!"

于是,狮子吃掉了兔子和松鼠。就这样,狮子一只一只地几乎吃掉了所有动物。

但狮子心想:"除了狐狸,所有的动物都来了。可为什么狐狸没有来呢?我又饿了,等等,我又听到了什么?"

这时就听见狐狸说:"狮子先生,您在里面吗?"

狮子暗暗高兴,狐狸终于还是来了,"是我,我在这儿。狐狸,请进吧。"

狐狸说:"我也想进去,先生。可是里面太挤了吧!"

狮子回答道:"这里面除了我,没有其他人啊。"

狐狸说:"真的吗?这洞穴口有这么多动物进去时留下的脚印,可是却没有一个走出来的脚印。那么,其他所有动物都在哪儿呢?"

The Old Lion

The Lion used to be the king of beasts. But now he was old and weak.

One day, the Rabbit said to the Squirrel, "Did you hear about the Lion? I heard he is very sick. How about visiting him?"

After they stepped inside the cave, then the Lion suddenly stood up and showed his teeth and claws.

The Rabbit shouted, "Let's get out!" The Lion said, "It's too late. You are trapped."

Then the Lion ate up the Rabbit and the Squirrel. The Lion ate up all of the animals in this way, one by one.

Then the Lion said, "All of the animals have come here except for the Fox. Why isn't the Fox coming? I'm getting hungry again. I hear something?"

The Fox asked, "Mr. Lion, are you in there?"

The Lion said, "Finally! It's the Fox. Yes, I'm in here, Fox. Come in."

The Fox replied, "I would like to, sir. But it's too crowded in there."

The Lion said, "There is no one in here but myself."

The Fox answered, "Really? There are many footprints going into your cave. But there are none coming out. Where are all of the other animals?"

狼来了

从前,有一个牧童在山上放羊。他无聊极了,便想捉弄一下大家。他冲着山下喊道:"狼来了!狼来了!救救我的羊。"

山下的村民听到牧童的呼叫,赶快冲上山,帮助他拯救羊群。可是他们一只狼都没看到。牧童只是看着他们愤怒的脸,捂嘴笑了起来。

"孩子,没有狼的时候,千万不要喊'狼来了'!"村民们生气地说着,然后离开了。

过了一会儿,牧童又觉得无聊,于是喊道:"狼来了!狼来了!"当村民们再次冲上山时,连狼的影子也没见到。随后,愤怒的村民们摇摇头,失望地下了山。

牧童继续看着羊群。过了一会儿,他看见一只狼朝着羊群走来,然后大声呼救。但是这一次,没有人来帮他。

到了晚上,牧童一直没有回家。村民们怕他出事,就上山去找他了,结果看见牧童坐在小山上哭泣。"我说有狼的时候,你们为什么不来?"他伤心地说,"我的羊都被狼吃掉了。"

The Boy Who Cried Wolf

Once upon a time, there lived a shepherd boy who was bored watching his flock of sheep on the hill. To amuse himself, he shouted, "Wolf! Wolf! Help me with my flock!"

The villagers came running to help the boy and save the sheep, but they found nothing and the boy just laughed as he looked at their angry faces.

"Boy, don't cry out 'Wolf! Wolf! Come and help' when there's no wolf!" they said angrily, and then they left.

After a while, he got bored and cried "Wolf!" again. The angry villagers warned the boy a second time and then went down the hill with disappointment.

The boy continued watching over the flock. After a while, he saw a wolf and shouted. But this time, no one came to help.

By the evening, when the boy did not return home, the villagers wondered what happened to him and went up the hill. The boy sat on the hill weeping. "Why didn't you come when I called out that there was a wolf?" he said sadly, "The whole flock was eaten up by wolf."

爱普莉月

有一个可爱的小女孩,她只有十岁,她的名字叫爱普莉。

一天,爱普莉问她的父母为什么叫她爱普莉。她母亲回答说,她叫爱普莉,是因为她出生在四月。小女孩听了很高兴。她喜欢自己的名字。

爱普莉也很喜欢四月,因为那个月是她的生日。她的父母为她举办了一个聚会,她所有的朋友都来和她一起庆祝,她还收到了很多礼物。

后来,她的妈妈怀孕了。很快,爱普莉就有了一个小弟弟。她的弟弟是二月份出生的。大家都来到爱普利家祝贺,并为新生儿的名字提出了建议。

爱普莉不明白问题出在哪里,这在她看来很简单,她说如果孩子出生在二月,名字就应该是二月!

April's Month

There was a nice little girl. She was 10 years old. Her name was April.

One day, April asked her parents why she was called April. Her mother answered that she was called April because she was born in April. The little girl was very happy to hear that. She liked her name.

April really liked the month of April, too. This was because she had her birthday in that month. Her parents gave her a party. All her friends came and celebrated with her, and she received a lot of presents.

Her mother became pregnant then, and soon April had a little brother. Her brother was born in February. Everyone came to visit the family. Everyone suggested names for the new baby.

April did not understand what the problem was. This seemed very simple to her. She said that if the baby was born in February, the name was February!

狐狸和小猫

一天,小猫在森林里遇到了狐狸,她很友好地和狐狸打招呼道:"早上好,亲爱的狐狸先生!你今天过得怎么样啊?"

狐狸傲慢不已,从头到脚打量了一下小猫,说道:"噢,你这只可怜的猫,你脑子里想的是什么?你怎么敢问我这样的问题,你精通几门技艺?"

"一门技艺。"小猫温顺地说。

"那是什么呢?"狐狸问。

"当狗追我的时候,我可以跳到树上救自己。"

"就仅仅是这些吗?"狐狸说。"我可是精通一百种本领。跟我来,我教你怎么从狗群里逃出来。"

就在这时,一个猎人带着四只猎狗走了过来。小猫麻利地跳上一棵树,蹑手蹑脚地爬到最上面的树枝上,被树枝和树叶全部遮住了。

说时迟那时快,猎狗咬住了狐狸,让他动弹不得。

小猫叫道:"狐狸先生,虽然你有一百种本领,而我只有一种本领,但是现在的我却安然无恙。如果你能爬到这儿来,你就不会被抓了。"

The Fox and the Cat

It happened once that the cat met the fox in the woods. She addressed him in a friendly manner. "Good morning, dear Mr. Fox! How is your day?"

The fox, full of pride, looked at the cat from head to foot for some time. At last he said: "Oh, you poor whisker-wiper. What has come into your head? How dare you ask me such a question? How many arts have you mastered?"

"Only one," said the cat meekly.

"And what might that one be?" asked the fox.

"When the dogs run after me, I can jump into a tree and save myself."

"Is that all?" said the fox. "I am master of a hundred arts. Come with me, and I will teach you how to escape from the dogs."

Just then a huntsman came along with four hounds. The cat sprang into a tree, and crept stealthily up to the topmost branch, where she was entirely hidden by twigs and leaves.

Within a minute, the dogs had gripped the fox, and held him fast.

"Oh, Mr. Fox!" cried the cat, "you, with your hundred arts, are in danger while I, with my only one, am safe. Had you been able to creep up here, you would not have lost your life."

狐狸和山羊

盛夏的一天,天气炎热,狐狸口渴了,到处找水喝。"今天真热,我好渴啊!"

突然,他发现了一口井,"这里有好多水呀,看起来凉爽又可口。我要怎么才能喝到呢?"

狐狸想了又想,"不管三七二十一,忍不住了,我要跳进去痛快喝一番。"

喝饱水的狐狸突然发现自己被困在井里出不去了。这时,一只找水喝的小山羊出现了。

狐狸对小羊说:"小山羊,快来试试这甘甜的井水吧,非常可口。"

小山羊在狐狸的指导下,纵身跳进了井里。

"嗯,真好喝!这是世界上最棒的水了,谢谢你让我跟你一起分享。"小山羊说道。

"没什么,我很高兴和你分享。不过你不觉得这里有点挤吗,既然我已经喝够了,要不我先出去,你多喝点?"狐狸建议道。

狐狸踩在小山羊的背上跳出了井口。

"狐狸,你在哪里呀?我喝完了,也想出去,请帮帮我。"小山羊请求道。

"对不起,小山羊,我不能帮你。如果我帮了你,我就出不去了。"狐狸边说边走开了。

The Fox and the Goat

It was a hot summer day. A thirsty fox was looking for water. "It's so hot today, and I'm so thirsty."

All of a sudden, he found a well, exclaiming, "There's lots of water here. It looks so cold and delicious. But how can I get the water?"

The fox thought, "I can't take it anymore. I'm too thirsty. I'll just jump in and have a splash."

Though fully satisfied with the well, the fox found himself trapped inside it. When he was almost turning desperate, a goat showed up.

The fox said to the goat, "Little goat, come and enjoy the juicy well water. It's super delicious."

The little goat jumped straight into the well under the fox's guidance.

"Yummy, so yummy. This is the best water in the world. Thank you for sharing this with me." the little goat said.

It's nothing. I'm just glad you like it. But don't you think it's too crowded in here? Since I am done with it, I should probably get out and leave you more space to enjoy more." the fox suggested.

The fox got onto the back of the little goat and stepped out of the well.

"Where are you, Fox? I'm done, too, and I want to get out as well. Can you help me?" the little goat begged for help.

"I'm sorry, little goat, I can't help you. If I do, I might fall in again."Said the fox, and he went away.

狗、公鸡和狐狸

狗和公鸡是一对最好的朋友，他们非常想见识一下这个世界。因此，他们决定离开农场。他们一路走着，没有遇到任何冒险的事。

傍晚时分，公鸡像往常一样找地方栖息，他发现附近有一棵空心树，觉得这棵树很适合过夜。狗可以爬进去，公鸡可以飞到其中一根树枝上，他们俩都可以睡得很舒服。

天刚亮，公鸡就醒了。他一时忘记了自己在什么地方，以为自己还在农场里，他有责任在天亮时把全农场的人叫醒。于是他踮起脚尖，拍着翅膀，使劲地叫着。他的叫声吵醒了森林里不远处的一只狐狸。

狐狸立刻幻想着一顿美味的早餐，他急忙跑到公鸡栖息的树下，很有礼貌地说："尊敬的先生，衷心欢迎您来到我们的森林。我无法表达我有多高兴能在这里见到您，我相信我们会成为最亲密的朋友。"

"我感到非常荣幸，善良的先生，"公鸡回答，"请你绕到我家门口，就在那棵树下，我的门房会让你进来的。"

这只饥肠辘辘的狐狸，听了公鸡的话，绕着树转了一圈，转眼间就被狗抓住了。

The Dog the Rooster and the Fox

Dog and Rooster who were the best of friends, wished very much to see something of the world. So they decided to leave the farmyard. They traveled along without meeting any adventure to speak of.

At nightfall, Rooster looking for a place to roost, as was his custom, spied a hollow tree nearby that he thought would do very nicely for a night's lodging. Dog could creep inside and Rooster would fly up on one of the branches, They slept very comfortably.

With the first glimmer of dawn, Rooster awoke. For the moment he forgot just where he was. He thought he was still in the farmyard where it had been his duty to arouse the household at daybreak. So standing on tip-toes he flapped his wings and crowed loudly. And he awakened Fox not far off in the wood.

Fox immediately had rosy visions of a very delicious breakfast. Hurrying to the tree where Rooster was roosting, he said very politely, "A hearty welcome to our woods, honored sir. I cannot tell you how glad I am to see you here. I am quite sure we will become the closest of friends."

"I feel highly flattered, kind sir," replied Rooster. "If you will please go around to the door of my house at the foot of the tree, my porter will let you in."

The hungry Fox went around the tree as he was told, and in a twinkling Dog had seized him.

守财奴和他的金子

从前,有个守财奴将他的金子埋到一棵树下,每周他都会去把金子挖出来看看。

一天晚上,一个小偷挖走了所有的金子。

守财奴再来查看时,发现除了一个空洞什么都没有了。守财奴震惊之余捶胸痛哭。他的哭声引来了所有的邻居,他把金子放在了哪里,以及他是如何每周来看金子的事情告诉了大家。其中一位邻居问:"你用过这些金子吗?"

"没用过,"他说,"我只是时常来看看。"

"那么,你以后常来看看这个洞,"这位邻居说,"就像以前有金子时一样。"

金句拾遗

Worship money like his life.
视财如命。

The Miser and His Gold

Once upon a time, there was a miser. He hid his gold under a tree, and he would visit the tree every week.

One night a robber stole all the gold under the tree.

When the miser came again, he found nothing but an empty hole. He was in shock, and then he burst into tears. Hearing the crying, all the neighbors came to gather around him. He told them where he kept the gold and how he used to come and visit his gold every week. "Did you ever take any of it out?" asked one of them.

"No," he said. "I only came to look at it."

"Then come to the hole again as usual," said the neighbor. "It will be the same just like before."

谁是你的守护天使

从前，有个孩子马上就要降生了。一天，他问上帝："听说明天您就送我去人间了，可我这么弱小和无助，我在那儿该怎么生活呢？"

上帝答道："在众多的天使中，我特别为你挑了一位。她会守候你，无微不至地照顾你。"

"如果我不懂人类的语言，他们对我说话时，我怎么听得懂呢？"孩子继续问道。

上帝轻轻地拍了一下孩子的脑袋，说："你的天使会对你说最最美丽、最最动听的话语，而这些都是你从未听过的。"

"听说人间有很多坏人，谁来保护我呢？"

"即使冒着生命危险，你的天使也会保护你的。"

此时，天堂一片宁静，人间的声音已可听到，他问了上帝最后一个问题，"上帝，假如我现在就出发，请你告诉我，我的天使叫什么名字？"

上帝把手放在小孩的肩上，答道："你的天使的名字很容易记住，你就叫她——妈妈。"

Who is Your Guardian Angel

Once upon a time, there was a child ready to be born. So one day he asked God, "They tell me that you are sending me to the Earth tomorrow, but how am I going to live there since I'm so vulnerable and helpless?"

God replied, "Among those many angels, I have chosen one for you. She will be there waiting for you and will take care of you."

"But how can I understand them when they talk to me," the child continued, "If I don't know the language they use?"

God patted him on the head and said, "Your angel will speak to you the most beautiful and sweetest language you will ever hear."

"I've heard on Earth there are bad men. Who is there to protect me?"

"Your angel will protect you even in the face of danger!"

At that moment the Heaven turned quite peaceful, and voices from the Earth could already be heard. He asked God one last question, "Oh God, since I am about to leave now, please tell me my angel's name."

God touched the child on the shoulder and answered, "Your angel's name is not hard to remember. You will simply call her Mama."

老鼠嫁女儿

很久很久以前,有一个老鼠爸爸,他想要将他的女儿嫁给世界上最伟大的人。

老鼠爸爸就去找太阳说话:"你好,太阳先生!我知道你是世界上最伟大的人,你愿意娶我的女儿吗?"

"我才不是世界上最伟大的人呢!最伟大的应该是云,只要他一出现,我就被遮住了。"太阳回答道。

于是老鼠爸爸去找云,"云先生!我知道你是世界上最伟大的人,你愿意娶我的女儿吗?"

"最伟大的应该是风,只要他一出现,我就被吹得远远的。"云说。

"风先生!我知道你是世界上最伟大的人,你愿意娶我的女儿吗?"

风说:"最伟大的应该是墙,只要他一出现,我就被挡住了。"

"墙先生!我知道你是世界上最伟大的人,你愿意娶我的女儿吗?""什么?最伟大的其实是你们老鼠!只要你们一出现,我就被挖出洞了!"墙先生吃惊地说。

老鼠爸爸好开心,他终于知道世界上最伟大的人就是老鼠。于是,他决定把自己的女儿嫁给隔壁英俊的鼠小弟。

The Mouse Marries off His Daughter

Once upon a time, there was a mouse father. He wanted to marry off his daughter to the greatest person in the world.

The mouse father went to talk to the Sun. "Hello! Mr. Sun. I know you are the greatest person in the world. Would you marry my daughter?"

"I'm not the greatest person in the world. The greatest person is the Cloud. If he comes out, I will be covered." the Sun said.

The mouse father went to talk to the Cloud. "Hello! Mr. Cloud, I know you are the greatest person in the world. Would you marry my daughter?"

"The greatest person is the Wind. If he comes out, I will be blown away." the Cloud said.

"Hello! Mr. Wind, I know you are the greatest person in the world. Would you marry my daughter?"

"The greatest person is the Wall. If he comes out, I will be stopped."

"Mr. Wall, I know you are the greatest person in the world. Would you marry my daughter?" "What? I'm not the greatest person in the world. The greatest person is YOU, the mouse. If a mouse comes out, I will be bitten a hole!" the Wall said surprisingly.

The mouse father was very happy. He finally knew that mice are the greatest person in the world. He would then marry his daughter to the handsome mouse next door.

小熊让路

一天,小熊打算独自一人去河对面的熊外婆家看望外婆。

去外婆家的路上必须要经过一座小桥,小桥非常窄,一次只能通过一个人。

小熊拎着篮子高高兴兴准备过桥,可是当他刚走到桥中央的时候,乌龟爷爷从对面走了上来。乌龟爷爷年纪大了,眼神不好使,腿脚也不方便,小熊便立刻从桥中央返回到桥头,好给乌龟爷爷让路。

乌龟爷爷走的速度很慢很慢……小熊便在桥头的另一边静静地耐心等待着乌龟爷爷走过来。走了好久好久,乌龟爷爷才走到桥的这边。

乌龟爷爷看见蹲在地上等着过桥的小熊,说道:"我们的小熊真是个耐心懂事的好孩子。"

小熊害羞地摸着自己毛茸茸的脑袋,笑着说道:"乌龟爷爷,这是我应该做的,并且十分乐意。"

Bear out of the Way

One day, Little Bear decided to go visit his grandma, whose home was located on the other side of the river.

He must cross over a small bridge in order to see her. The bridge was extremely narrow and it only allowed one to pass at a time.

Carrying a basket in his hand, Little Bear departed. When he was in the middle of the bridge, Grandpa Turtle showed up. Grandpa Turtle was old in age and he had decreased vision in his eyes. His legs were weak and was unable to walk properly. Having seen this, Little Bear stared to retreat in order to give way to Grandpa Turtle.

Grandpa Turtle walked very, very slowly... Nevertheless, Little Bear patiently waited for Grandpa Turtle's to come through first. It took Grandpa Turtle a few hours to arrive at the other side of the bridge.

When Grandpa Turtle saw Little Bear squatting on the ground, waiting. Grandpa Turtle said, "Our Little Bear is such a patient and sensible boy."

Little Bear smiled shyly and touched his furry head, saying, " Grandpa Turtle, this is what I should do, with pleasure. "

顽强的小兔

最近，小兔跟着小马老师学习长跑。一天，小马老师领着小兔一边跑一边进行讲解，他们穿过了一片小树林，又越过了一座小山。不久，小兔就累得汗流浃背了，她多么希望能够停下来好好休息一会儿啊。

就在这时，小兔一不小心被一个木桩狠狠地绊倒在地上。这一下可摔得不轻，连新衣服都磕破了，小兔痛得大哭了起来。

小马老师听到哭声马上返了回来，给她做了检查，并说："小兔，不要害怕，坚持才能胜利。如果碰到一点儿小困难就退缩，肯定失败。你要坚强！"

听了小马老师的话，小兔从地上慢慢站了起来。树上的鹦鹉也鼓励道："小兔，加油！你一定会成功的。"小兔点了点头，擦干眼泪继续向前跑。

就这样，经过自己的努力，小兔在夏天的森林马拉松比赛中赢得了长跑冠军！

Persistent Little Rabbit

Little Rabbit has been learning how to run with Teacher Horse lately. One day, Teacher Horse led Little Rabbit on a quick run, while showing her how to run better. They went through a small wood and then over a small hill. Very quickly, Little Rabbit became all sweaty and tired, hoping that she could stop and have a rest.

Just then, Little Rabbit got tripped over a wooden post by accident and fell onto the ground. It was a bad fall and her clothes got ripped. Little Rabbit was hurt badly and began to cry out aloud.

Teacher Horse heard her crying and returned to check her up. He said, "Little Rabbit. Don't be scared. Hold on. You shouldn't give up so easy even if you run into difficulties. Stay strong."

After hearing what Teacher Horse's words, Little Rabbit got up slowly. The Parrot in the tree also encouraged her, saying, " Little Rabbit, come on! You will succeed." Little Rabbit nodded Yes. After drying her tears, Little Rabbit went on running again.

Having made tremendous efforts, Little Rabbit eventually won the Summer Marathon Championship.

矮婆婆的树皮小屋

在森林深处有一个用树皮搭成的小屋子，里面住着矮婆婆。

一天，高婆婆来矮婆婆家玩，她的脚刚跨进门，"砰"，头就撞在了门框上。矮婆婆抱歉地说："对不起，对不起，我的房子太矮了。"第二天，胖婆婆也来矮婆婆的家里玩，但因为她身子太胖，被门卡住了，怎么也进不去。

没有朋友登门与自己聊天，矮婆婆觉得无比孤单。

一天，一群小朋友在森林里玩的时候发现了树皮小屋，他们高兴地叫起来："多像童话故事里的小屋啊！真漂亮！"

矮婆婆邀请小朋友们坐在小椅子上，不高也不矮，坐着真舒服！矮婆婆又端出自己做的又香又甜的蛋糕请小朋友们吃。小朋友们在矮婆婆家的墙上画了好多漂亮的画，有的画了美丽的花蝴蝶，有的画了神气的大公鸡。

矮婆婆的树皮小屋变成了小朋友们最喜欢的地方。有了孩子们的笑声，矮婆婆再也不觉得孤单了。

Grandma Short's Hut

In the depths of the forest, there is a hut made of tree bark, where Grandma Short lived.

One day, Grandma Tall came to visit Grandma Short. Just when she was about to step into the hut, she banged her head on the door frame. Grandma Short felt really sorry for that, apologizing, " I'm sorry, my door is too short for you to enter." The next day, when Grandma Chubby came to visit Grandma Short, she got stuck by the door because her body was too big and wide.

No one came to visit Grandma Short and she felt an extreme pain of loneliness.

One day, a bunch of children playing in the forest, discovered the hut. They happily screamed to one another, " What a beautiful hut ! It looks like it's from a fairy tale."

Grandma Short invited the children to come in and take a seat. Those chairs are neither tall nor short. It's so comfortable to sit in. Grandma Short also brought out the sweet and yummy cake she made for the children to eat. The children also painted a lot of beautiful pictures on the wall, some painted beautiful butterflies while others painted big roosters.

Grandma Short's little hut became the children's favorite place. Surrounded by the sound of children's laughter, Grandma Short never felt alone again.

想长大的小青蛙

有一天,小青蛙对妈妈说:"妈妈,我也想和您一样出去工作。"青蛙妈妈回答道:"可是你还没有长大呀。"

小青蛙不服气,趁着青蛙妈妈不注意悄悄溜了出去。来到外面的世界,小青蛙乱了手脚,不知道自己该做什么。看到青蛙伯伯正在工作,小青蛙学着他们的样子捉起了害虫。直到傍晚,小青蛙才带着一袋子的害虫回到家。这时,他已经累得精疲力尽。

小青蛙看到妈妈,说:"妈妈,妈妈,我现在总算知道了,长大可真累啊!"

妈妈笑着说:"既然长大这么累,那你现在还想长大吗?"

小青蛙说:"想!"

妈妈有点儿惊讶:"为什么呀?"

小青蛙说:"因为长大了就能帮妈妈分担辛苦了呀!"

金句拾遗

As a man sows, so shall he reap.
种瓜得瓜,种豆得豆。

Little Frog Wants to Grow up

One day, Little Frog said to his mother, "Mom, I want to go out to work just like you." Mother Frog replied, "But you haven't grown up yet."

Little Frog was, however, not convinced and quietly slipped out when Mother Frog was not paying attention. Coming into the outside world, Little Frog got slightly freaked out and had no idea what to do. After observing what other Uncle Frogs were doing at work, Little Frog started to learn from them. He worked very hard until evening and went home with a bag of pests, completely exhausted.

Seeing his mother, Little Frog said, "Mom, Mom. Now I've come to realize that growing up can be exhausting!"

Mother Frog smiled and said, "Since growing up is so tired, do you still want to grow up now?"

Little Frog said, "Yes absolutely!"

Mother Frog replied, a little surprisingly, "Why?"

Little Frog said, "Because when I grow up, I can help you out more and share the hard work!"

听 Wanderer 老师
读英文故事

傲慢的玫瑰花

花园里,有一朵非常漂亮的玫瑰花,她骄傲地认为自己是世上最美的花。

每当人们路过这里,都会情不自禁地低下头来,闻一闻她的芳香,并且赞美她几句。过了不久,玫瑰花身旁长出一株狗尾草,玫瑰花生气地说:"你是谁?离我远点!"

"我是新落户的邻居,希望我们成为好朋友。"狗尾草礼貌地回答。

玫瑰花厌恶地说:"你长得这么难看,想跟我成为好朋友,想都别想!"狗尾草难过地低下了头。

不过,为了生存,不管玫瑰花多么嫌弃和讨厌自己,狗尾草每天都很努力地让自己的根往深处扎。

很快,夏天来了,接连很多天都没下一滴雨。玫瑰花因为汲取不到充足的水分,渐渐地枯萎了,而狗尾草却因为扎根很深,依然可以在风中快乐地舞蹈。

金句拾遗

Pride hurts, modesty benefits.
满招损,谦受益。

The Arrogant Rose

In the garden, there is a very beautiful rose flower, which proudly considered herself the most beautiful flower in the world.

Every time people pass by, they can't help but bow their heads, smell the fragrance, and praise her a few words. Soon after, an green fox-tail grows side by side with the rose. The rose says angrily, "Who are you? Stay away from me!"

"I am a newly settled neighbor and hope we can become good friends." The green fox-tail responds politely.

Rose says in disgust, "You look so ugly. Don't you ever think of being my friend!" the green fox-tail lowers her head sadly.

But in order to survive, no matter how much the rose dislikes and loathes her, the green fox-tail works hard every day to reach deep underneath the ground.

Sooner or later, when summer comes and there comes a few days when there is not a drop of rain. The rose flower gradually withers because it couldn't absorb enough water, however the green fox-tail stands still and dances happily in the wind because of its deep roots.

勇于承认错误的小象

牛大叔辛辛苦苦在地里忙了整整一年,好不容易眼看自己种的玉米就要丰收了,可不知道是哪个淘气的家伙,把就要丰收的玉米踩得乱七八糟,牛大叔伤心得在田地里哭泣。

这件事被动物们知道了,大家决定一起找出这个淘气的家伙,好好地教训他一顿。

小象听到这个消息,吓得躲在家里不敢出门。

象妈妈奇怪地问小象说:"孩子,你怎么不出去跟伙伴们一起玩,躲在家里干什么?"

小象"哇哇"大哭起来,说:"我错了!牛大叔的玉米是我弄坏的,我和小狗在玉米地里比赛跑,压坏了牛大叔地里的玉米。"

象妈妈说:"那你应该去跟牛大叔道歉,真心的歉意是会被原谅的。"

小象听了妈妈的话,去牛大叔家道歉了。

后来,牛大叔原谅了小象,还夸他是个勇于承认错误的好孩子。

小象为了弥补自己的过失,决定帮助牛大叔一起种玉米。

Little Elephant Owns up Mistakes

Uncle Ox has worked very hard in the field for a whole year. When he was, finally, about to harvest the corn stalks, he found that the corn field was trampled to a complete mess, Uncle Ox was heart-broken, sobbing in the filed.

This incident was quickly known to the other animals, and they all decided to find out who this abhorrent troublemaker was and gave him a lesson.

Upon hearing the news, Little Elephant became so scared that he dared not to go out.

Mother Elephant curiously asked Little Elephant, "Little Elephant, why don't you go out and play with your friends? Why are you hiding up?"

Little Elephant cried out aloud, " It's my bad. Uncle Ox's corn field was damaged by me. I was playing with Little Dog in the field. We were running in the field. I trampled on the filed and crushed everything. "

Mother Elephant said, " Then you should apologize to Uncle Ox. A sincere apology will be forgiven."

Little Elephant listened to her mother and went to Uncle Ox's house to apologize.

In the end, Uncle Ox forgave Little Elephant and also praised him as a good and honest boy, owing up to mistakes.

In order to make it up to Uncle Ox, Little Elephant decided to help Uncle Ox grow corn together.

小袋鼠让座

海海和洋洋是袋鼠妈妈的一对小宝贝。星期天,他们高高兴兴跟妈妈乘车去看姥姥。

刚上车时,车上人少,他们坐上了舒舒服服的座位。渐渐地,车上的人多了起来。

这时,羊公公、鸡婆婆也上了车,可这时车上早就没有空座位了,羊公公和鸡婆婆只好站着。海海和洋洋想起幼儿园里鹿阿姨的话:"要尊敬长辈,做好孩子!"

海海和洋洋离开座位,异口同声地说:"羊公公、鸡婆婆,你们请坐吧!"

"不!你们还小,还是你们坐吧!"羊公公说。

"羊公公,你们坐吧!"袋鼠妈妈一边招呼着羊公公和鸡婆婆,一边搂住海海和洋洋,说:"宝贝,来,到妈妈怀里来!"

海海和洋洋跳进妈妈胸前的大口袋里,再也挤不着了。他们虽然看不见外面的好风光,可心里甜甜的。听!羊公公、鸡婆婆正在夸他们是懂礼貌的好孩子呢!

Little Kangaroo Offering Seats

Haihai and Yangyang are Mother Kangaroo's baby twins. On Sunday, they happily went on a bus to see their grandma with Mother Kangaroo.

When they first got on the bus, there were few people. They took a comfortable seat and sat down. Gradually, the bus started to become crowded.

At this time, Grandpa Goat and Grandma Chicken got onto the bus, however there were no longer any seats available. Grandpa Goat and Grandma Chicken had no choice but to stand on the bus. Haihai and Yangyang recalled what Aunt Deer said at the kindergarten, "Respect the elderly and be good."

Haihai and Yangyang said, " Grandpa Goat and Grandma Chicken, please have a seat!"

"No! You are still young. You should sit down!" said Grandpa Goat.

"Grandpa Goat, please sit down!" Mother Kangaroo greeted they while wrapping her arms around Haihai and Yangyang, "Come, come to mama's arms."

Haihai and Yangyang quickly jumped into the big pocket on Mother Kangaroo's chest. Although they couldn't see the beautiful scenery outside, they were warm inside. Listen! Grandpa Goat and Grandma Chicken are praising them for their good manners.

妈妈最辛苦

熊妈妈买回来了一张按摩椅,熊宝贝和熊爸爸都抢着往上坐。熊妈妈想出一个好办法,说:"你们父子俩谁表现好,谁是家里最辛苦的,就先让谁来坐。"

第二天,熊宝贝就拿出100分的成绩单说:"妈妈看,这是我辛苦得来的100分。"

熊妈妈摸摸熊宝贝的头,说:"嗯,真乖。"

这时,熊爸爸赶紧凑了过来,说:"我今天下班后帮你做家务,把家里打扫得干干净净。"

熊妈妈为难了起来,不知道该选谁,她决定让熊宝贝和熊爸爸再比一场。

第三天,过了晚餐时间,熊妈妈还没有回家。熊宝贝和熊爸爸很着急。这时,他们看见熊妈妈大包小包拎着很多东西回了家,熊宝贝问:"妈妈,这都是什么啊?"

熊妈妈说:"这是今天晚上的菜,这是日用品,这是给你和爸爸买的新衣服。"

熊宝贝和熊爸爸看着每天打扫卫生、洗衣做饭、照顾自己的熊妈妈,立刻拉着熊妈妈坐在了按摩椅上。他们觉得,每天为家里默默付出的熊妈妈才是最辛苦的。

Mama Works the Hardest

Mama Bear bought a massage chair. Baby Bear and Daddy Bear both wanted to sit on it first. Mama Bear has a good idea,"Whoever behaves the best and works the hardest, will be the winner. And the winner gets to sit on the massage chair first.

The next day, Baby Bear took out a score report of 100 points and said, "Mom, this is 100 points from working hard."

Mama Bear touched Baby Bear's head and said, "Well done."

Daddy Bear hurriedly added , I came home from work today and have thoroughly cleaned the house."

Mama Bear was caught in a dilemma, not knowing who to choose. She decided to create another compctition.

On the third day, after dinner time, Mama Bear was still not home. Baby Bear and Daddy Bear became worried and anxious. At this time, they saw Mama Bear returning home with bags full of stuff. Baby Bear asked, "Mom, what are these?"

Mama Bear said, "This is the food for tonight and these are daily necessities. Those are the new clothes I bought for you and your dad."

Baby Bear and Daddy Bear both recalled Mama Bear cleaning the house, doing the laundries and cooking for them every single day. They decided to offer the massage chair to Mama Bear instead because they recognized that the Mama Bear worked the hardest in the house.

鹬蚌相争

一天，一只河蚌得意洋洋地张开壳，在河滩上晒太阳。有一只鹬鸟恰好从河蚌身边走过，就去啄河蚌的肉。这时候，河蚌急忙把壳合上，紧紧地夹住了鹬鸟的喙。鹬鸟用尽力气，也拔不出自己的喙。而河蚌也脱不了身，不能回到河里去。

河蚌和鹬鸟就争吵了起来。鹬鸟气呼呼地说："一天不下雨，两天不下雨，没有了水，你回不了河里，总是要干掉的。"

河蚌也气呼呼地说："一天不放你，两天不放你，你的喙拔不出来，也别想活。"

河蚌和鹬鸟谁也不让谁，吵个不停。这时候，有个渔夫提着渔网，沿着河边走来。看见鹬鸟和河蚌相持不下，他非常高兴，毫不费力地把它们两个一齐捉住，塞进鱼篓里带回家去了。

The Snipe Grapples with the Clam

One day, a clam proudly opened its shells to sunbathe itself on the river bank. A snipe passed by the clam and stretched its bill to peck at the clam's flesh. The clam hurriedly closed its shells and tightly grasped the snipe's bill between them. Despite all its efforts, the snipe could not extricate its bill. At the same time, the clam could not let go of himself and returned to the river either.

Then the clam and the snipe began to quarrel. The snipe said angrily, "If it doesn't rain for a day or two, there will be no water. Since you can't return to the river, then surely you will die anyway."

The clam also said angrily, "If I don't discharge you for another day or two, you won't be able to pull out your bill. Don't even think about staying alive."

Neither the clam nor the snipe would give in, and they kept on grappling. At this moment, a fisherman came along the riverside with a fishing net. He was very glad to see the snipe and the clam at a deadlock. Without the least effort, he caught them both, put them into his fish basket and carried them home.

拔苗助长

古时候，在宋国有一个农夫，他的性格很急躁，自从春耕播种以后，他就天天到地里去看秧苗，盼着它们长得又高又壮。有一天他去地里锄草，看到自己家的秧苗比别人的都要矮一些。他心想：这秧苗长得太慢了，我得想办法帮它长得快一些。但是怎样才能使秧苗长高呢？

为这事，他愁得吃不好饭，睡不好觉。终于，他想出了办法：把秧苗往上拔一拔，让它快点长高！说干就干，他偷偷下田去把秧苗一棵一棵拔高，拔完一垄又一垄，累得汗流浃背，腰酸腿疼。他疲惫不堪地回到家里，躺在炕上长嘘了一口气，兴奋地对他的儿子说："今天可把我累坏了，我帮助秧苗长高了好几寸。"

儿子听到父亲这么一说，心里想：秧苗怎么会无缘无故长高呢？真是奇怪，不行，我得去看一下。于是，他拔腿就往田里跑。等他跑到田边一看，发现秧苗都开始枯萎了。

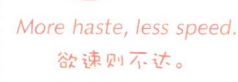

More haste, less speed.
欲速则不达。

Pulling Up the Seedlings to Help Them Grow

In ancient times, there was once a man in the State of Song who had an impatient disposition. Day and night he longed for the seedlings in the field to grow tall and strong. One day, while he was working in the field, he noticed that the seedlings in his field were shorter than those of the neighbors. He said to himself,"The seedlings has been growing too slowly. I have to come up with a plan to make it grow faster. What can I do to make it grow faster?"

Due to his desperation, neither could he sleep well, nor eat well. Eventually, he came up with an idea. Why can't I pull it a little bit up and help it grow? He sneaked to the field and started pulling each seedling up a little bit from the soil. Seeing that all these seedlings in the field were taller than before, he felt very pleased with himself. He went home, though all worn out, he felt really happy and shared with his son. "I have worked for like a whole day today. How tired I am! But the seedlings in the field have grown a lot taller."

Upon hearing what his father had said, the son started wondering,"How come the seedlings decide to grow taller? This is so weird. I have to go check it out." He dashed to the filed, and found that all the seedlings have started to wither.

南辕北辙

从前有一个人,计划从魏国到楚国去。他带了很多的路费,雇了上好的马车,请了驾车技术精湛的车夫,就上路了。

路上有人问他要往哪儿去,他大声回答说:"去楚国!"路人告诉他说:"到楚国去应往南方走,你这是在往北走,方向不对。"

他满不在乎地说:"没关系,我的马快着呢!"路人替他着急,拉住他的马,阻止他,说:"方向错了,你的马再快,也到不了楚国呀!"他说:"不要紧的,我带的路费多着呢!"路人极力劝阻他,说:"虽说你路费多,可你走的不是那个方向,路费再多也只是白花呀!"

他有些不耐烦地说:"这有什么难的,我的车夫赶车的本领高着呢!"路人无奈,只好松开马车,看着他离去。

那个魏国人,不听别人的指点劝告,仗着自己的马快、钱多、车夫好等优越条件,朝着相反方向一意孤行。

Going South by Driving the Carriage North

There was once a man who planned a trip from the State of Wei to the State of Chu. He carried with him enough money, hired a good carriage with an excellent car-man and was ready to depart.

Someone met him on the road asked him where he was heading to? He replied loudly, "Go to the State of Chu!" The passerby told him, "You actually should go south if your destination is in the State of Chu. Now that you are going north, you are apparently heading in the wrong direction."

He said indifferently, "It doesn't matter. My horse is fast!" The passerby got a little concerned, grabbed his horse, and stopped him halfway, saying, " No matter how fast your horse is, if the direction is opposite, there is no way you can get to the State of Chu!" The man said unconsciously,"I have a lot of travel expenses!" Passersby tried to dissuade him from keep going further. "Although you have a lot of travel expenses, you are not heading in the right direction. Your money will be wasted! "

He said: "It can't be so difficult. My car-man is highly skillful!" The passerby had no choice but to let go of his carriage, watching him disappear in the distance.

The man refused to listen to other people's advises. He blindly relied on such things as fast horses, good fortune, and excellent car-man, but refused to believe in the fact that he was going in the opposite direction.

孔融让梨

从前有个名叫孔融的孩子,十分聪明懂事。孔融有五个哥哥,一个弟弟,兄弟七人相处得十分融洽。

有一天,孔融的母亲买来许多梨,哥哥们让孔融和最小的弟弟先拿。

孔融看了看盘子中的梨,发现梨有大有小。他不挑好的,不拣大的,只拿了一只最小的梨,津津有味地吃了起来。

父亲看见孔融的行为,十分高兴,心想:别看这孩子还小,却懂得应该把好的东西留给别人的道理呢。于是,他故意问孔融:"盘子里这么多的梨,又让你先拿,你为什么不拿大的,只拿一个最小的呢?"孔融回答说:"我年纪小,应该拿个最小的,大的应该留给哥哥吃。"

父亲接着问道:"弟弟不是比你还小吗?照你这么说,他应该拿最小的一个才对呀?"

孔融说:"我比弟弟大,我是哥哥,我应该把大的留给小弟弟吃。"

父亲听他这么说,大笑着说:"你真是一个好孩子!"

Kong Rong Shares the Pears

There was a child named Kong Rong, who was very smart and sensible. Kong Rong has five elder brothers, one younger brother. The seven brothers lived happily together.

One day, Kong Rong's mother bought many pears and brought home for the brothers to eat. Brothers let Kong Rong and the youngest brother to pick first.

Kong Rong looked at the pears on the plate and found that there were big pears and small pears. Neither did he pick the best one, nor did he pick the biggest one. Instead, he picked the smallest pear and started to eat with relish.

Father saw what Kong Rong did and was very pleased with him. He thought to himself,"even though he is just a kid, he understands that he should give good things to others first."Then he deliberately asked Kong Rong, "There are so many pears on the plate. Why don't you take the big one and why did you only take the smallest one?" Kong Rong replied, "I'm younger. I should take the smallest one and leave the bigger ones to my brothers."

Father followed up and asked, " But your brother is younger than you? Based on what you said, he should eat the smallest one?"

Kong Rong said, "I am older than my younger brother. I am his older brother. I should offer the bigger one to my younger brother. "

After hearing what he said, Father burst into laughter," You are such a good boy!"

猴子捞月

一群猴子在林子里嬉戏，其中一只小猴子跑到一口井旁玩耍，他趴在井沿往下一看，忽然大叫起来："不得了啦，月亮掉到井里去了！"原来，小猴子看到井里有个月亮。

一只大猴子听到叫声，忙带着一群猴子跑到井边，朝井里一看，也吃了一惊，跟着大叫起来："糟了，糟了，月亮掉到井里去啦！"

他们的叫声惊动了猴群，老猴子带着一大群猴子朝井边跑来。当他们看到井里的月亮时，一起惊叫起来："哎呀，糟了！月亮真的掉到井里去了！"

老猴子说："我们快想办法把月亮捞起来吧！"猴子们都同意老猴子的建议，加入到捞月亮的队伍中。

井旁边有一棵老槐树，老猴子率先跳到树上，自己头朝下倒挂在树上，其他的猴子就依次一个一个你抱我的腿，我勾你的脖子，挂成一长条，头朝下一直深入井中。小猴子最轻，所以挂在最下边。快到井底时，只听见他对其他猴子喊："行了，够得着了。"

小猴子把手伸到水里去捞月亮,井水给他一搅,月亮碎成一片一片在水里摇曳。小猴子吓得喊了起来:"不好了,月亮让我抓破了!"

大家议论纷纷,都不知该如何是好。

不一会儿,井水慢慢平静了,又出现了又圆又亮的月亮。小猴子高兴地喊:"月亮又圆了!"小猴子又伸手去捞,捞了半天,还是只捞到一把水。小猴子捞不到月亮,急得吱吱直叫:"月亮一碰就破,再也捞不起来啦!"

小猴子这么一叫,倒挂了半天的猴子们觉得很累,都有点支撑不住了。这时候,老猴子忽然抬头一看,又圆又亮的月亮还好好地挂在天上呢,就对大家说:"你们看,月亮不是好好地挂在天上吗?井里的是月亮的影子。傻孩子,快上来看月亮吧!"

听老猴子这么一说,小猴子、大猴子,一个一个都爬了上来。大家看着又圆又亮的月亮,都吱吱吱吱地笑了起来。

The Monkeys and the Moon

A group of monkeys were playing in the forest. One of the monkeys ran away to play by a well. The little monkey rested on the edge of the well, suddenly shouted, "This is bad! The moon had fallen into the well!" It turned out that the little monkey saw a moon inside the well. A big monkey heard the sound, ran to the well with a group of monkeys. They looked inside the well, then was startled, yelling together, "Very bad! The moon fell into the well!"

Their calls alarmed the group, and the older monkey ran towards the well with a larger group of monkeys. When they saw the moon inside the well, they all screamed together, "It's over! The moon really fell into the well!"

The older monkey said, " Let's find a way to get the moon out of the well!" All the monkeys agreed with the older monkey's suggestion and joined the "rescue team".

There was an old locust tree next to the well. The old monkey took the lead to jump onto the tree, hanging himself upside down and then he pulled the next monkey's feet with his hands. All the other monkeys followed the suit-one monkey after another, hanging themselves upside down till they almost reached the bottom of the well. Since the little monkey was the lightest of all, he was the last one on the monkey chain, he yelled out to other monkeys from the bottom of the well, "Enough! I'm almost here."

As the little monkey reached into the water to catch the moon, the water got stirred by his hands and the moon was shattered into pieces. I have damaged the moon."

All the monkeys started to discuss what to do next.

After a short while, the water slowly became peaceful once more, and moon reappeared. The little monkey shouted happily, "The moon has changed back and turned round again!" The little monkey reached out to get the moon again. He tried again and again and did that for a while, but nothing happened. All he got was water in his hands. The little monkey couldn't catch the moon and squeaked anxiously, "The moon would break into pieces as long as I touch it! We can never get it!"

The little monkey's screaming has made all the monkeys feel exhausted, and they couldn't hold onto it any longer. At this time, the older monkey looked up, the moon was still hanging in the sky. "Look, isn't the moon hanging in the sky? That was the shadow of the moon inside the well. Silly boys, come up and see the moon from here!"

After hearing what the older monkey said, all the other monkeys started climbing up one after another. They all looked at the round and bright moon and began giggling.

听 Wanderer 老师
读英文故事

愚公移山

古时候,有位老人名叫愚公。他家的门口有两座大山,一座叫太行山,一座叫王屋山,一家人进出非常不方便。

一天,愚公对全家人说:"这两座大山挡在了咱们家的门口,进出很不方便。咱们全家出力,移走这两座大山,大家觉得如何?"

他的儿子、孙子一听,都说:"您说得对,咱们明天就开始干!"

其他人也都说:"只要我们一起努力干,就一定能够移走这两座大山。山上的石头和泥土,我们可以填放到海里去。"

第二天,愚公带着一家人开始搬山了。隔壁邻居嘲笑他说:"你这么大岁数了,路也走不动了,能搬得动山吗?"

愚公乐观地回答他:"虽然我年纪已大,但是我还有儿子,还有孙子。而山上的石头却是搬走一点儿就少一点儿,我们每天这样不停地搬,为什么不能搬走山呢?"

愚公带领一家人每天起早摸黑挖山不止,终于感动了天帝。天帝派了两个神仙下凡,把这两座大山搬走了。

Yu Gong Wants to Remove Mountains

In the ancient times, there was an old man named Yu Gong. There were two big mountains in front of his house, one called TaiHang Mountain and the other called WangWu Mountain. The two big mountains made it rather inconvenient for Yu Gong's whole family to come and go.

One day, Yu Gong said to his whole family, "These two mountains are blocking the entrance to our house. It is very inconvenient to enter and exit. Let's all contribute and removes the two mountains. What do you think?"

His sons and grandsons all agreed, "You are right. Let's do it from tomorrow onward!"

Everyone else responded, "As long as we work hard together, we will be able to remove these two mountains. The stones and mud can be used for reclamation."

The next day, Yu Gong and his family began to remove the mountain. Their neighbor saw it and laughed at him, "You are so old and you can barely walk. How can you possibly remove mountains?"

Yu Gong told him with optimism, "Although I am old, I still have sons and grandchildren, and this could pass down to my next generations. The stones from the mountains therefore would become less. If we continue doing this everyday, how can we not succeed in removing the mountains?"

Yu Gong led his whole family everyday from morning to evening in order to remove the mountain, and his motivation finally moved God. God sent two goddesses from the heaven to the earth and helped them remove the two mountains away.

年的传说

很久很久以前,有一个吃人怪兽叫作"年"。它常年住在深海里,只有在农历的最后一天,天气转暖,春天快到来的时候它才会出现。村民们都很害怕它。

有一年,一个旅行者来到了镇上,寻找食物和栖身之处。只有一位老太太给他提供了帮助,其他人都忙着逃命。为了感谢老太太,旅行者告诉了她驱除年兽的秘密。

那天晚上,当年兽到达他们村庄时,除了老太太外,其他人都跑到山上去了,街道上空无一人。当年兽正要靠近老太太家门的时候,里面传出震耳欲聋的爆竹声,这可把年兽吓坏了。年兽看到房子上贴满了红纸,吓得落荒而逃。村民们回来的时候,看到老太太毫发无伤,便询问了她缘由。

从此以后,每当到了年兽出没的日子,村民们便整晚不睡,聚在一起点爆竹,在房屋周围点上红灯笼,在墙壁、门上贴满红纸,穿上红衣服,伴着嘹亮的音乐声载歌载舞。

从那时起,年兽就再也没有回来过。慢慢地,这个传统一直延续下来,并逐渐演变成我们的中国新年。

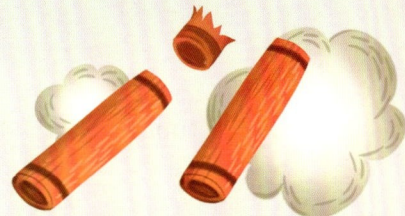

The Story of Nian

A long long time ago, there was a cannibal monster called Nian. It lived under the deep sea all year round, and only appeared on the last day of the lunar year when the weather got warmer and when the spring was coming. The villagers were all very afraid of Nian.

One year, a traveler came to town to find food and shelter. There was only an old lady who was willing to offer him help while others were busy running away for their lives. In order to thank the old lady, he told her a secret to expel cannibal monster Nian.

On the night, when the beast reached their village, all villagers except the old lady, ran up the hill to hide up, and the streets were empty. When the beast was about to approach the old lady's front door, there came a deafening sound of firecrackers. The sound scared the crap out of the monster. The monster saw that the house was covered with red paper. Nian was so scared that he ran away immediately. When the villagers came back, they saw the old woman unharmed and asked her what had happened.

Since then, every time around which the beast was about to come out and feast on people, the villagers would stay awake all night, gather around to set off firecrackers, light up red lanterns around their houses, stick red paper on the walls and doors, wear red clothes, and sing and dance along with loud music.

听 Wanderer 老师
读英文故事

From then now, Nian slowly disappeared and never showed up again. But the tradition kept on and has gradually evolved into our Chinese New Year.

东郭先生和狼

从前,有一位东郭先生。一天,他牵着毛驴出门去市场。忽然,一只神色慌张的狼蹿了出来说:"先生,您快救救我吧!猎人在后面就要追上来了,您把我藏在您的口袋里吧!"

听了这话,东郭先生的心就软了,答应了狼的请求。

这时,猎人追上来了,问东郭先生:"您有没有看见一只狼?"东郭先生故作镇定地说:"没看见。"

等猎人走远了,东郭先生长舒了一口气,把狼放了出来。

狼一边舒展着身体,一边恶狠狠地对东郭先生说:"先生,我现在可是饿坏了,你心肠这么好,就让我吃了你吧!"东郭先生又怕又气,嘴里喊着:"你这只恶狼,我刚才好心救了你的命,你现在却要吃我!"

就在这个危急的时刻,来了一位拄着拐杖的老人。东郭先生赶忙拉住老人,把刚才发生的一切讲了一遍。狼也开始为自己辩解着。

老人想了想,说:"你们都认为自己有理。这样吧,你们把刚才的情形再示范一遍让我看看。"

狼觉得老人说的话有理,就又钻进了东郭先生的口袋里,东郭先生立刻把袋口系紧了。老人举起拐杖狠狠地朝狼打去。

Mr. Dong Guo and the Wolf

Once upon a time, there was a gentleman called Mr. Dong Guo. One day, he led his donkey to the market. Suddenly, a panicked wolf jumped out, terrifying, "Sir, please help me! The hunter is after me! Would you please hide me in your pocket!"

After hearing his plea, Mr. Dong Guo's felt touched and he agreed to the wolf's request.

At this time, the hunter came up and asked Mr. Dong Guo, "Did you see a wolf ?" Mr. Dong Guo shook his head calmly and said, "I didn't see it, I didn't see it."

When the hunter went away, Mr. Dong Guo took a sigh of relief, untied the bag, and released the wolf.

While stretching his body, the wolf said viciously, "Sir, I am hungry now. You have a good heart. Let me eat you to satisfy my hunger." Mr. Dong Guo was frightened and angry, and he shouted,"You evil wolf ! I was kind enough to have saved your life just now, but now you want to devour me!"

At this critical moment, an old man with crutches came. Mr. Dong Guo hurriedly grabbed onto the old man, explained what had happened just now. The wolf began to defend himself too.

The old man thought for a while and said, "Both of you think that you are the more reasonable one, you should demonstrate again what really had happened just now."

Wolf agreed with old man, and jumped into Mr. Dong Guo's pocket again. Mr. Dong Guo tightened up the pocket immediately. The old man raised his cane and started hitting the wolf fiercely.

田螺姑娘

从前,有一位勤恳能干的单身汉,一天他在田间劳作的时候拾到一只大田螺。他将这枚田螺带回家,养在了水缸里。转眼三年时间过去了。

一天,单身汉在田里忙活了一整天。回到家后,他发现桌子上摆满了热气腾腾的饭菜。他肚子饿极了,便狼吞虎咽地吃了起来。他边吃边想,会是谁给他煮这么好吃的一桌饭菜呢?

第二天,单身汉干完活回到家,发现饭桌上又摆满了丰盛的饭菜,连茶壶里的开水都烧好了。

连续几天都是如此,这让单身汉感到非常奇怪,他决定要弄个明白。

一天,他假装去田地干活,半路上却偷偷回了家。躲在门后的他发现厨房水缸的盖子忽然打开了,从里面走出一位美丽的姑娘。她走到灶台边,做起饭来。原来,每天给他做饭的就是这位美丽的姑娘。

一问才知道,这位姑娘原来是一位田螺仙女,因前世单身汉救过她的命,今生又养了她三年,她是投身来报恩的。后来,单身汉和田螺姑娘结了婚,幸福快乐地生活在一起了。

The Snail Girl

Back in the old days, a diligent and capable bachelor found a big snail while working in the field one day. He took the snail back home and kept it in the water tank. Three years have gone by.

One day, after a busy day toiling away in the field, the bachelor returned home and found that hot meals were nicely prepared on the dinner table. He was so hungry that he started digging in the minute he saw the food. While he was eating, he wondered who could it be to have prepared all these for him?

The next day, the same thing happened again. After the bachelor returned home from work, he saw food on the table again and even the teapot was filled with hot water.

The same thing happened again and again in the following few days, which prompted the curious bachelor to find out what's going on.

One day, he pretended to have gone to the fields for work, but secretly returned home halfway to find out what's really happening. When he was hiding behind the door, he found that the lid of the kitchen water tank suddenly opened, and a beautiful girl stepped out of it. She went to the stove, started cooking. It turned out that this beautiful girl was the one who kept cooking for him every day.

After some inquires, he found out that this girl was a fairy. Since the bachelor had saved her life in the previous life, and raised her for three years in this life, She was there to repay. In due course, the bachelor and the girl got married and happily lived forever.

守株待兔

从前，宋国有个农夫，家里种着几亩地，在他的农田边有一棵大树。一天，他在地里干活，忽然看见一只兔子箭一般地飞奔过来，猛地撞在那棵大树上，一下子把脖子撞断了，当场就死了。

这个农夫飞快地跑过去，把兔子捡起来，高兴地说："这真是一点儿劲没费，白捡了个大便宜，回去可以美美地吃上一顿了。"他拎着兔子一边往家走，一边得意地想："我的运气真好，没准明天还会有兔子跑来。"

第二天，他来到地里，什么活也不干，专门守着那棵大树，等着兔子撞过来。结果，他等了一天什么也没等到。但是他并不甘心，从此以后每天都到那棵大树下等。他等呀等呀，直等到地里的野草长得比庄稼都高了，却连个兔影都没有再见到。

Waiting for Rabbits by the Tree

There was once a farmer from the State of Song, where he cultivated several acres of farmland, and next to the farmland, there stood a huge tree. One day, while he was toiling away in the field, he saw a rabbit making a dart for his direction and slamming into the big tree. The rabbit broke his neck on the dot and died on the spot.

The farmer quickly rushed over so that he could keep the rabbit to himself. The farmer said happily, "This is really effortless. What a steal! Now I can go home to enjoy my delicious rabbit dish now." While he was carrying the dead rabbit home, he said to himself with a pride, "Luck is on my side. Perhaps there will be another rabbit dropping dead in front of me."

On the following day, he went to the field again, however, with no intentions to work at all. He decided to dedicate himself to the tree, waiting for the rabbit to show up again. In the end, nothing appeared. But he was not ready to give up. From this day onwards, he would spend his whole day under the big tree. He waited and waited until the weeds in the ground grew even taller than the crops. Unfortunately, there was nothing at all, not even the shadow of a rabbit.

听Wanderer老师
读英文故事

十二生肖的故事

很久很久以前,天神玉帝说:"我们要选十二种动物作为人的生肖,一年一种动物。定好一个日子,动物们来报名,就选先到的十二种动物为十二生肖。"

消息一公布,动物们纷纷各自准备起来。猫和老鼠是邻居,又是好朋友,他们都想去报名。猫说:"咱们得一早起来去报名,可是我爱睡懒觉,怎么办呢?"老鼠说:"你尽管睡你的大觉,我一醒来,就去叫你,咱们一块儿去。"

报名那天,老鼠起得很早,牛也起得很早,他们在路上碰到了。牛走得很快,老鼠也跑得上气不接下气,但还是落在牛的后面。

老鼠心里想路还远着呢,我快跑不动了,这可怎么办?他脑子一动,想出个主意来,就对牛说:"牛哥哥,我来给你唱个歌。"牛说:"好啊,你唱吧。咦,你怎么不唱呀?"

老鼠说:"我在唱哩,你没听见吗?哦,可能是我的嗓门太小了,你没听见。这样吧,让我骑在你的脖子上,唱起歌来你就能听见了。"

牛说:"好嘞!"小老鼠就沿着牛腿一直爬上了牛脖子,让牛驮着他走,可舒服了。

当牛跑到报名的地方一看,谁也没来,高兴得昂昂地叫起来:"我是第一名!"牛还没把话说完,只见老鼠从牛脖子上一蹦,蹦到地上,哧溜一下蹿到牛前面去了。结果是老鼠得了第一名,牛得了第二名。所以,在十二生肖里,小小的老鼠排在最前面。

后来又陆续来了好多动物,按照他们的报名顺序,十二生肖依次是:鼠、牛、虎、兔、龙、蛇、马、羊、猴、鸡、狗、猪。

猫呢,十二生肖中怎么没有猫?原来,报名那天早晨,老鼠早早就醒来了,可是他光想着赶快去报名,把叫猫起床的事忘得一干二净,就自己去报名了。结果,老鼠被选上了,猫因为睡懒觉,起床晚了,等他赶到时,十二种动物已被选定了。

The Story of the Zodiac

Long long time ago, the Heavenly God Jade Emperor said, "We have to choose twelve animals as the zodiac, one animal a year. So, let's set a day. we allow all animals to come and register. Whoever comes first, will be picked as the zodiac."

As soon as the news was announced, the animals began to prepare themselves for the day of selection. Cat and Mouse were neighbors and also good friends. They both wanted to participate in the registration. The Cat said, "We have to get up really early to register, but I am used to getting up late. What should I do?" The mouse said, "Don't worry. You can sleep as usual and I will wake up. We can go together."

On the day of registration, Mouse got up really early and so did Cow. They ran into one another on the road. Cow walked very quickly, Mouse was almost out of breath, but still fell behind Cow.

Since there was still a long way to go and now he could barely walk any more, Mouse started wondering what he could do to get there eventually. He came up with an idea, and said to Cow, "Brother Cow, I'll sing a song for you." Cow said, "Okay, go ahead...emm why don't you sing?"

Mouse said, "I'm singing. Why can't you hear it. Maybe it's because my voice is low and you couldn't hear it. How about this? Let me ride on your neck to sing for you. That way, you wouldn't miss it?"

Cow said, "Sounds good!" Mouse quickly climbed onto the Cow's neck from along side his legs and rode on his neck, which was very comfortable.

When Cow arrived at the registration place, nobody was there yet. He shouted happily, "I am the first one!" Not having finished what he was saying, Mouse quickly got off from his neck, jumped in front of him and claimed the first place. Cow turned out to be the second one. Therefore, in the Chinese zodiac, Mouse has ranked No.1. Sooner or later, a lot other animals showed up.

According to the order of their registration, the zodiac signs are - Mouse, Cow, Tiger, Rabbit, Dragon, Snake, Horse, Sheep, Monkey, Chicken, Dog and Pig.

As for cats, why are there no cats in the Chinese zodiac? It turned out on the morning of the registration day, Mouse got up early for the registration, but he completely forgot to wake up Cat. In the end, he left home all by himself instead. As a result, Mouse was selected. Cat woke up late and by the time he arrived at the registration place, all twelve animals had already been selected.

聪明的小象

一天,小松鼠在森林里玩耍,一不小心掉入了一个大坑。"救命啊,救命啊……"小松鼠拼命地呼喊道。就在这时,小鸟看到了,急忙去搬救兵。

第一个到的救兵是小猴,他尝试着用长长的木棍把小松鼠捞上来,可是怎么也捞不上来,因为小松鼠怎么都抓不住木棍。接着,小熊也赶到了。他提着一桶水往坑里倒,可是坑太大了,水桶又太小,要倒到什么时候才能救出小松鼠呢?

大家正绞尽脑汁想办法的时候,小象急匆匆地赶来了,说:"还是看我的吧!"

于是小动物们看到小象把长长的鼻子伸进了大坑里,只见他用大鼻子把小松鼠卷了起来。

"小松鼠得救了,小松鼠得救了!"大伙儿高兴极了,一齐欢呼起来。被捞起来的小松鼠谢过了小象,夸他是森林里最聪明的小象!

A Smart Elephant

One day, while playing in the forest, the little squirrel accidentally fell into a big pit. "Help, help …" the Little Squirrel cried desperately. At this moment, the bird saw it and hurried off to get the rescuers.

The first rescuer was Monkey. He tried to pick up the Little Squirrel with a long wooden stick. The Little Squirrel couldn't hold onto the stick. Then the bear also arrived. He carried a bucket of water and started pouring water into the pit. But the pit was too large to be fully filled with water. When would be it an end?

When everyone was racking their brains to find a way, the baby elephant hurriedly came and said, "Let me try!"

Then all the animals saw the little elephant put his long nose into the giant pit, only to find that he quickly rolled up the little squirrel with his big nose.

"The little squirrel is saved! The little squirrel is saved!" Everyone was very happy and cheering together. The little squirrel thanked the baby elephant and praised him as the smartest elephant in the forest!

听 Wanderer 老师
读英文故事

我的妈妈

这是我妈妈,她真的很棒啊!

我妈妈是个手艺超群的大厨师,

也是一个很会杂耍的"特技演员"。

她不但是个神奇的画家,

还是全世界最有力气的女人!

我的好妈妈,真呀真棒呀!

我妈妈是一个有魔法的园丁,

她能让所有的东西都生长得非常好看。

她也是一个善良的仙女,

我难过时,她总是把我哄得很开心。

她的歌声像天使一样甜美,

我的好妈妈,真呀真棒呀!

我妈妈像蝴蝶一样美丽,

也像猫咪一样温柔,

我的好妈妈,真呀真棒呀!

不管我妈妈是个舞蹈家,还是个航天员,

也不管她是个电影明星,还是个清洁工,

她都是我的好妈妈!

我妈妈是一个超人妈妈,

常常逗得我哈哈大笑。

我爱我妈妈,而且你知道吗?

她也爱我!(永远爱我。)

My Mum

She's nice, my mum.

My mum's a fantastic cook, and a brilliant juggler.

She's a great painter, and the strongest woman in the world!

She's really nice, my mum.

My mum's a magic gardener.

She can make anything grow.

And she's a good fairy.

When I'm sad she can make me happy.

She can sing like an angel.

She's really, really nice, my mum.

My mum's as beautiful as a butterfly.

She's as soft as a kitten,

She's really, really really nice, my mum.

My mum could be a dancer, or an astronaut.

She could be a film star, or the cleaner.

But she's my mum.

She's a super-mum! And she makes me laugh. A lot.

I love my mum. And you know what?

She loves me ! (And she always will.)

秋千

你喜不喜欢荡秋千?

荡着秋千飞上蓝天?

在小孩子的世界里,这是最快乐的游玩!

飞向空中,越过围墙,我看到天地如此宽广,

河流、树木、牛群和所有的一切,勾画着这美丽的村庄。

我低头看见绿葱葱的花园,脚下面还有棕色的屋顶,

我荡着秋千又飞上天,飞上飞下不厌倦!

金句拾遗

Do as the Romans do.
入乡随俗。

The Swing

How do you like to go up in a swing,

Up in the air so blue?

Oh, I do think it the pleasantest thing

Ever a child can do!

Up in the air and over the wall,

Till I can see so wide,

Rivers and trees and cattle and all

Over the countryside.

Till I look down on the garden green,

Down on the roof so brown.

Up in the air I go flying again,

Up in the air and down!

你是我的阳光

你是我的阳光，我唯一的阳光

当天空是灰暗的时候，你让我内心充满阳光

亲爱的，你从不知道，我是多么爱你

请不要，把我的阳光带走

你是我的阳光，我唯一的阳光

当天空是灰暗的时候，你让我内心充满阳光

亲爱的，你从不知道，我是多么爱你

请不要，把我的阳光带走

You are my sunshine

You are my sunshine

My only sunshine

You make me happy

When skies are gray

You never know, dear

How much I love you

Please don't take

My sunshine away

You are my sunshine

My only sunshine

You make me happy

When skies are gray

You never know, dear

How much I love you

Please don't take

My sunshine away

我们同在一起

当我们同在一起,

在一起,在一起,

当我们同在一起,

其快乐无比。

你的朋友就是我的朋友,

而我的朋友就是你的朋友,

当我们同在一起,

其快乐无比。

当我们同在一起,

在一起,在一起,

当我们同在一起,

其快乐无比。

你的朋友就是我的朋友,

而我的朋友就是你的朋友,

当我们同在一起,

其快乐无比。

当我们同在一起,

在一起,在一起,

当我们同在一起,

其快乐无比。

The More We Get Together

The more we get together,
Together, together,
The more we get together,
The happier we'll be.

For your friends are my friends,
And my friends are your friends.
The more we get together,
The happier we'll be!

The more we get together,
Together, together,
The more we get together,
The happier we'll be.

For your friends are my friends,
And my friends are your friends.
The more we get together,
The happier we'll be!

The more we get together,
Together, together,
The more we get together,
The happier we'll be.

萤火虫

小小流萤,

在树林里,在黑沉沉暮色里,

你多么快乐地展开你的翅膀!

你在欢乐中倾注了你的心。

你不是太阳,你不是月亮,

难道你的乐趣就少了几分?

你完成了你的生存,

你点亮了你自己的灯;

你所有的都是你自己的,

你对谁也不负债蒙恩;

你仅仅服从了你内在的力量。

你冲破了黑暗的束缚,

你微小,但你并不渺小,

因为宇宙间一切光芒,

都是你的亲人。

——[印度]泰戈尔

Fireflies

Little fireflies, in the woods, in the dark twilight, how happy you to spread your wings!

You in joy into your heart.

You are not the sun, you are the moon, are you the pleasure of a bit less? Have you finished your existence, you light your lamp;

You are all of your own, you who have no debt favor;

You just obey

Your inner strength.

You broke through the darkness,

you are small, but you are not small,

because the universe of all light,

all your loved ones.

———[India] Tagore

小鸟在说些什么

小鸟在说些什么呢,

在这黎明初晓的小巢中?

小鸟说,让我飞吧。

妈妈,让我飞走吧。

宝贝,请多留片刻,

待到你的小翅膀初长成。

小鸟又多留了一会儿,

然而它还是飞走了。

What does Little Birdie Say

What does little birdie say,

In her nest at peep of day?

Let me fly, says little birdie,

Mother, let me fly away.

Birdie, rest a little longer,

Till the little wings are stronger.

So she rests a little longer,

Then she flies away.

纸船

我每天把纸船一个个放在急流的溪中。

我用大黑字写我的名字和我住的村名在纸船上。

我希望住在异地的人会得到这纸船,

知道我是谁。

我把园中长的秀利花载在我的小船上,

希望这些黎明开的花能在夜里被平平安安地带到岸上。

我投我的纸船到水里,

仰望天空,

看见小朵的云正在张着满鼓着风的白帆。

我不知道天上有我的什么游伴把这些船放下来同我的船比赛!

夜来了,我的脸埋在手臂里,

梦见我的纸船在子夜的星光下缓缓地浮泛前去。

睡仙坐在船里,带着满载着梦的篮子。

——[印度]泰戈尔

Paper Boats

Day by day I float my paper boats one by one down the running stream.

In big black letters I write my name on them and the name of the village where I live.

I hope that someone in some strange land will find them and know who I am.

I load my little boats with shiuli flower from our garden,

and hope that these blooms of the dawn will be carried safely to land in the night.

I launch my paper boats and look up into the sky

and see the little clouds setting thee white bulging sails.

I know not what playmate of mine in the sky sends them down

the air to race with my boats!

When night comes I bury my face in my arms

and dream that my paper boats float on and on under the midnight stars.

The fairies of sleep are sailing in them, and the lading ins

their baskets full of dreams.

——[India]Tagore

晴天或阴天

无论是晴天或是阴天,

无论是冷天或是暖日,

不管喜欢与否,我们都要学会经受人生的风霜雨露。

听 Wanderer 老师
读英文故事

Sunny or Cloudy

Whether the weather be fine or whether the weather be not.

Whether the weather be cold or whether the weather be hot.

We'll weather the weather whether we like it or not.

酸菜

彼德·派柏拿起一撮泡好的酸菜。

一撮泡好的酸菜是被彼德·派柏拿起来的。

如果彼德·派柏拿起来一撮泡好的酸菜,

那么彼德·派柏拿起的泡好的酸菜在哪儿呢?

Pickled Peppers

Peter Piper picked a peck of pickled peppers.

A peck of pickled peppers Peter Piper picked.

If Peter Piper picked a peck of pickled peppers,

Where's the peck of pickled peppers Peter Piper picked?

季节歌

小伙伴们!你们知道四个季节是什么吗?

是春天,夏天,秋天和冬天!

我们唱一首关于季节的歌儿吧!

春天,夏天,秋天,冬天,

秋天,冬天,

秋天,冬天,

春天,夏天,秋天,冬天。

你最喜欢什么季节呢?

我喜欢春天的郁金香!

春天很美丽!

我喜欢夏天的樱桃!

它们多汁美味!

我喜欢秋天的板栗!

它们香甜好味道!

我喜欢冬天的雪!

真冷呀!

春天,夏天,秋天,冬天,

秋天,冬天,

秋天,冬天,

春天,夏天,秋天,冬天。

你最喜欢什么季节呢?

我喜欢冬天!

The Seasons Song

Hello, do you know what the four seasons are?

They are Spring, Summer, Fall and Winter!

Let's sing a song about the seasons!

Spring, summer, fall, winter,

Fall, winter,

Fall, winter,

Spring, summer, fall, winter,

What's your favorite season?

I like tulips in the spring?

They're beautiful!

I like cherries in the summer!

They're juicy!

I like chestnuts in the fall!

They're yummy!

I like snow in the winter!

It's cold!

Spring, summer, fall, winter

Fall, winter,

Fall, winter,

Spring, summer, fall, winter,

What's your favorite season?

I like winter!

来到车站

大清早,我们来到火车站,

看到喷气小火车排成排,

看到火车司机拉开小把手。

嚓嚓!嚓嚓!嚓嚓!

我们出发啦!

大清早,到了公交车站,

看到忙碌的公交车排成排,

看到公交车司机呼喊着乘客。

嘀!嘀!嘀!

我们出发啦!

Down by the Station

Down by the station, early in the morning,

See the little puffer trains, all in a row,

See the engine driver,Pull the little handle.

CHUFF!CHUFF!CHUFF!

And off we go!

Down by the station,early in the morning,

See the busy buses,all in a row,

See the bus driver calling to the passengers.

BRRM! BRRM! BRRM!

And off we go!

变戏法

把你的右脚伸出去,把你的右脚收回来。

把你的右脚伸出去,然后一直摇摆着右脚。

你变着戏法,自己再转个圈。

你做得真棒呀!

把你的右手伸出去,把你的右手收回来。

把你的右手伸出去,然后一直摇摆着右手。

你变着戏法,自己再转个圈。

你做得真棒呀!

把你的头伸出去,把你的头收回来。

把你的头伸出去,然后一直摇摆着头。

你变着戏法,自己再转个圈。

你做得真棒呀!

把你的整个身体向前,把你的整个身体向后。

把你的整个身体向前,然后一直扭动整个身体。

你变着戏法,自己再转个圈。

你做得真棒呀!

The Hokey Pokey

You put your right foot in, you put your right foot out.

You put your right foot in, and you shake it all about.

You do the Hokey Pokey and you turn yourself around.

That's what it's all about.

You put your right hand in, you put your right hand out.

You put your right hand in, and you shake it all about.

You do the Hokey Pokey and you turn yourself around.

That's what it's all about.

You put your head in, you put your head out.

You put your head in, and you shake it all about.

You do the Hokey Pokey and you turn yourself around.

That's what it's all about.

You put your whole self in, you put your whole self out.

You put your whole self in, and you shake it all about.

You do the Hokey Pokey and you turn yourself around.

That's what it's all about.

听 Wanderer 老师
读英文故事

回家路上不停歌唱

回家路上不停歌唱,

结束了一天的时光。

回家路上不停歌唱,

看着影子渐渐远去。

不论遇到了什么都要保持微笑,

它会照亮你回家的路,

减轻你的负担,

如果你在回家的路上不停歌唱。

金句拾遗

All roads lead to Rome.
条条大路通罗马。

回家路上不停歌唱,

结束了一天的时光。

回家路上不停歌唱,

看着影子渐渐远去。

不论遇到了什么都要保持微笑,

它会照亮你回家的路,

减轻你的负担,

如果你在回家的路上不停歌唱。

Sing Your Way Home

Sing your way home,
At the close of the day.
Sing your way home,
Drive the shadows away.
Smile every mile for wherever you roam,
It will brighten your road,
It will lighten your load,
If you sing your way home.

Sing your way home,
At the close of the day.
Sing your way home,
Drive the shadows away.
Smile every mile for wherever you roam,
It will brighten your road,
It will lighten your load,
If you sing your way home.

听 Wanderer 老师
读英文故事

动物园一日游

我们要去动物园啦!

看看大象甩着它长长的象鼻,

大大的耳朵和不断摆动的长长象鼻。

看看猴子们不停地挠痒,

跳来跳去不停地挠痒,

长长的尾巴垂下来。

所有的海豹都在泳池里欢快地叫着,

它们会抓鱼会欢快地叫喊,

所有的小海豹也都欢快地叫着。

我们玩了一整天,我有点疲倦了,

坐在汽车里我睡着了,

还没到家就已经睡熟了,

我们可是玩了一整天啊!

Going to the Zoo

We're goin' to the zoo!

See the elephant with the long trunk swingin',

Great big ears and a long trunk swingin'.

See all the monkeys they're scritch scritch scratchin',

Jumpin' around and scritch scritch scratchin',

Hangin' by the long-tail huff huff huff.

Well the seals in the pool all honk-honk-honkin',

Catchin' the fish and honk-honk-honkin',

Little tiny seals all honk-honk-honkin'.

Well we stayed all day and I'm gettin' sleepy,

Sittin' in the car gettin' sleep,

Home already gettin' sleep sleep sleepy,

Cause we have stayed all day!

图书在版编目（CIP）数据

宝贝，一起读双语胎教故事 / 万娘娘编著 . — 北京：中国轻工业出版社，2022.3

（睡前胎教系列）

ISBN 978-7-5184-3217-2

Ⅰ . ①宝… Ⅱ . ①万… Ⅲ . ①胎教－基本知识 ②儿童故事－作品集－世界 Ⅳ . ① G610.8 ② I18

中国版本图书馆 CIP 数据核字（2020）第 190333 号

责任编辑：秦　功　巴丽华

策划编辑：秦　功　　　　　责任终审：劳国强　　版式设计：奥视读乐
封面设计：奥视读乐　　　　责任校对：晋　洁　　责任监印：张京华

出版发行：中国轻工业出版社（北京东长安街 6 号，邮编：100740）

印　　刷：北京博海升彩色印刷有限公司

经　　销：各地新华书店

版　　次：2022 年 3 月第 1 版第 2 次印刷

开　　本：889×1194　1/24　印张：6

字　　数：95 千字

书　　号：ISBN 978-7-5184-3217-2　定价：39.80 元

邮购电话：010-65241695

发行电话：010-85119835　传真：85113293

网　　址：http://www.chlip.com.cn

Email：club@chlip.com.cn

如发现图书残缺请与我社邮购联系调换

220305S3C102ZBW